Henry Wood

The Red Court Farm

A novel. Vol. 2

Henry Wood

The Red Court Farm
A novel. Vol. 2

ISBN/EAN: 9783337245337

Printed in Europe, USA, Canada, Australia, Japan

Cover: Foto ©Andreas Hilbeck / pixelio.de

More available books at **www.hansebooks.com**

THE

RED COURT FARM.

A Novel.

BY

MRS. HENRY WOOD,

AUTHOR OF

"EAST LYNNE," ETC. ETC.

IN THREE VOLUMES.

VOL. III.

LONDON :

TINSLEY, BROTHERS, 18 CATHERINE STREET, STRAND.

1868.

LONDON:
SAVILL, EDWARDS AND CO., PRINTERS, CHANDOS STREET,
COVENT GARDEN.

CONTENTS

OF

THE THIRD VOLUME.

THE RED COURT FARM.

CHAPTER I.

THE week went on to its close. Mary Anne Thornycroft, following out her own will and pleasure, despising her brother Cyril's warning, asked Robert Hunter to prolong his visit. He yielded so far as to defer his departure to the Sunday evening. Originally it had been fixed for the Saturday morning : business required his presence in London. Swayed by her, and by his own inclination—by his own love, he yielded to the tempting seduction of staying two further days. Alas, alas !

Peace had been established at the Red Court Farm ; or, rather, the unpleasantness had been allowed to die away. Nothing further had come of the outbreak ; it was not alluded to again in any way. Robert Hunter, meeting the super-

intendent, mentioned in a casual manner that
he could not help him again in sounding the
rocks, adding something about "want of time."
It is probable that the surprise caused by the
very unexpected arrival of Mr. Thornycroft's wife
tended more than aught else to smooth matters.
A stranger in our household keeps down angry
tempers. Isaac and Cyril were courteous as ever;
the justice was courteous also, though a little
stiff; Richard sternly civil.   Robert Hunter
responded cordially, as if willing to do away with
the impression left by his interference, and took
things as he found them.

Not a word was said of the newly-avowed love.
Any sort of concealment or dishonour was entirely against the nature of Mary Anne Thornycroft; but love was all-powerful.   That Robert
Hunter was not in a condition to propose for her
yet, he knew; but if this project of going abroad
were carried out, he thought he might speak before starting.   And so they mutually decided to
wait—at least, for a few weeks, or until that
should be decided.   But, though Mr. Thornycroft had not a suspicion of any attachment, the
brothers were sharper sighted.   They saw it
clearly, and showed disapproval in accordance

with their several dispositions. Richard resented
it; Isaac told his sister she might do much
better; Cyril said a word to her of concealment
never bringing any good. It was rather singular
that a dislike of Robert Hunter should exist in
the breast of all three. Not one, save Richard, acknowledged it even to himself; not one could say
whence or wherefore it arose, except perhaps that
they had not taken cordially to him at first. And
of course the outbreak did not tend to improve
the feeling.

The arrival of Lady Ellis at the Red Court
made no difference whatever to the routine of its
daily life, since she was not well enough to come
down and mix in it. The artificial excitement
imparted by the journey was telling upon her
now, and her available strength seemed to have
gone. Not tracing this fact—the increased weakness—to its true source, she laid the blame on
the atmosphere of Coastdown. It never had
agreed with her, she said; she supposed it never
would; and she already began to speak of getting
back to Cheltenham. Not rising until nearly
mid-day, she went afterwards into the dressing-
room, or boudoir, adjoining her chamber—we
saw her in it once in the old days—and there sat

1—2

or lay for the rest of the day, watching the mysterious plateau and the sea beyond it, or reading
between whiles. They went up and sat with her
by turns—Mr. Thornycroft, Cyril, and Mary
Anne; Isaac rarely, Richard never, except for a
brief moment of civil inquiry. None of them
remained with her long. It wearied her to converse, and she thought she was best with her
maid, who was in part companion. Robert
Hunter she neither saw nor asked after. And
so the week came to an end.

Sunday—and the day of Mr. Hunter's departure. They attended church at St. Peter's in
the morning, all except Mr. Thornycroft and
Richard. The justice remained with his wife,
and Richard was lax at the best of times in
attendance on public worship. Mr. Richard
spent the morning in a desultory manner at home,
a short pipe in his mouth, and lounging about
the stables with Hyde.

What Richard did with himself in the afternoon nobody knew; it was not usual to inquire
into his movements; but the rest went over to
Jutpoint to attend the church of St. Andrew's,
where there was a famous afternoon preacher,
whom they liked to hear. Anna Chester was

with them. Captain Copp, confined to the house
by a temporary indisposition, was indoors that
day, and his wife remained in attendance on
him; so that Anna appeared at church in the
morning alone. The Red Court people took her
home and kept her to luncheon; and she accom-
panied them afterwards to Jutpoint.

The omnibus conveyed them, and was to bring
them home again. Never, when he could avoid
it, did Mr. Thornycroft take out his own horses
on Sunday: he chose that they and his servants
should, so far, have rest. They had a large
circle of acquaintances at Jutpoint, and on
coming out of church the justice and Isaac laid
hands on two, and conveyed them back to dinner.
The strangers liked these impromptu invitations
—possibly laid themselves out to get them, and
the omnibus had a merry freight back to Coastdown.

"If they are going to have one of their din-
ner-gatherings to-night, you must come home
and sit down to it with me, Anna," spoke Miss
Thornycroft, as they quitted the omnibus at the
Mermaid.

Anna was nothing loth. She had sat in the
omnibus by Isaac's side, her hand in his, under

cover of the closely-packed company and the approaching darkness, happy for the time. Hastily answering that she would be glad to come, but must run on first of all to the heath and tell Mrs. Copp, she sped away fast. Isaac, having waited until the others should disperse before he followed, overtook her just as she was entering.

Captain Copp, up now, sat by the fire, groaning, and drinking some strong tea. The captain was occasionally afflicted with an intense sickheadache, never a worse than that he had to-day. He always laid the blame on the weather; it was the heat, or it was the cold; or it was the frost, or the rain. Mrs. Copp agreed with him, but Sarah in the kitchen thought the cause lay in rum-and-water. The groans were suspended when they went in, and Mrs. Copp, dutifully waiting on him, put down the cup and saucer.

"Aunt, may I dine at the Red Court?"

Mrs. Copp made no answer. Whenever she saw Isaac and Anna together, she was taken with a fit of inward shivering. Captain Copp spoke up: his opinion was that Anna had better not. Isaac laughed.

"She must," he said; "I am come to run

away with her. Otherwise Mary Anne will not sit down to table with us."

" Is it a party ?" cried the captain.

" Just two or three. My father has brought them over from Jutpoint; and I think Kyne is coming in. I was in hopes you could have come, captain."

Several dismal groans from Captain Copp. He said it was the pain in his head; in reality they sprung from pain at his heart. One of those glorious dinners at the Red Court, and he unable to be at it!

" Are you ready, Anna ?" whispered Isaac.

She ran upstairs to get something she wanted in the shape of dress, and was down again in a minute, wishing them good evening. Captain Copp, who did not altogether approve of the proceeding, called out that he should send Sarah for her at eight o'clock.

Taking her arm within his, Isaac walked on in silence. At the close of the heath, instead of continuing his way down by the side of the church-yard, he turned into it by the small side gate.

" Just a minute, Anna," he said, sitting down on the narrow bench. " I want to say a word to you."

But before he began to say the word he enclosed her face in his loving arms, and took the kisses from it he had been longing for all the way from Jutpoint.

"What I want to say is this, Anna, that I do not think I can let the present state of things go on."

"No!"

"It is so unsatisfactory. My wife, and not my wife. I living at the Red Court, you secluded at Captain Copp's. Meeting once in a way in a formal manner, shaking hands and parting again, nothing more. Why, I have only twice I think had you for a moment to myself since we parted, now and that evening at the Red Court. And what was *that*?—what is *this*? I can't stand it, Anna."

"But what would you do?"

"I don't know," answered Isaac, looking straight forward at the gravestones, as if they could tell him what. "I would brave my father's anger in a minute if it were not for—for—if I were sure nothing would come of it. But it might."

"In what way?"

"I may tell you some time; not now. If

Captain Copp would but be reasonable, so that I might entrust him with the secret, and———"

"He .would go straight off with it to Mr. Thornycroft, Isaac."

"Precisely," said Isaac, answering her interruption; "and the time has hardly arrived for that. Besides, the information must come from myself. Do you think———"

"Hush, Isaac!"

The softly-breathed warning silenced him. On the other side the hedge was a sound of footsteps — slow steps passing towards the heath. Isaac held her to him in perfect silence until they were lost in the distance.

"Let us go, Isaac."

It certainly would not be expedient to be seen there, and Isaac rose, snatching as he did so his farewell kisses from her lips. Passing down the side path of the churchyard, they went out at its front entrance, and popped upon Mr. Kyne.

He was evidently coming from the heath. It might have been his footsteps they had heard going towards it. Mr. Kyne looked full at them, and Anna coloured in the night's darkness to the very roots of her hair. To be caught at that hour stealing out of the churchyard with Isaac Thornycroft !

"Is it you, Mr. Supervisor?" cried Isaac, gaily. " A fine evening ! Take care, Miss Chester : you had better take my arm."

" It's very fine," answered the supervisor; " the weather seems to have cleared up. I've been taking a stroll before my tea. We shall have a frost to-night, Miss Chester."

" Safe to," rejoined Isaac, looking up at the clear sky.

" How is my lady?" asked Mr. Kyne; " I heard she had come."

" She has only come to go again. Coastdown never seems to suit her. She is very unwell indeed, and keeps her room."

The churchyard past, Mr. Kyne, without any warning whatever, turned off on the cross path towards his home, saying goodnight. Isaac looked after him in a sort of surprise.

" Then Richard *has* left it to me," he said, half aloud.

" Isaac ! Isaac ! what will Mr. Kyne think of me?" murmured Anna.

Isaac laughed. " The most he can think is

that we are sweethearts," he answered in his light manner.

" Oh, Isaac, have you considered ? If scandal should arise !"

" My darling, I have told you why that cannot be. At the first breath of it I should avow the truth. Scandal ! how is it possible, when we are living here but as common acquaintances ?"

At the gate of the Red Court he let her enter alone, and ran back in search of Mr. Kyne. That functionary lodged at a cottage just beyond the village, and Isaac found him poking up his small fire to make the little tin kettle boil, preparatory to making his tea.

" I have come to carry you off to dinner," said Isaac. " We have got a friend or two dropped in from Jutpoint, and the parson's coming. There's a brave codfish and turkey."

Weak tea and bread-and-butter at home in his poor small room ; and the handsome dinner table, the light, the warmth, the social friends at Justice Thornycroft's. It was a wide contrast, making Mr. Kyne's mouth water. He had dined at one o'clock off a mutton chop, and was hungry again. Codfish and turkey !

" I'll come with pleasure, Mr. Isaac. I must

just say a word to Puffer first, if there's time."

"All right; I'll go with you," said Isaac.

Mr. Puffer, the coastguard-man for the night, was on the plateau, speculating upon how long it would be before daylight was *quite* gone, for a streak or two of yellow lingered yet in the west, when he was surprised by the sight of his superior, and began to pace the edge zealously, his eyes critically peering out to sea. The supervisor approached alone.

"Any news, Puffer?"

"None, sir," answered Mr. Puffer, saluting his master. "All's quiet."

"Very good. Keep a sharp look-out. I shall be up here again at seven or eight o'clock."

He had taken to say this to his men of late, by way of keeping them to their duty; he had also taken to pop upon them at all kinds of unpromised times: and, between the cold and the superstition, his men wished him at Hanover.

The party sat down to dinner at six. Richard came in with Mr. Hopley, from Dartfield, who was wont to come over to buy oats; the parson of the parish, Mr. Southall, was there; the gentlemen from Jutpoint, and Mr. Kyne. A jolly parson, Mr. Southall, who enjoyed the good cheer of the Red Court Farm on Sunday just as much as he did on week days, and made no scruple over it.

The only two in strict evening dress were Robert Hunter and Cyril Thornycroft; but they wore black neckties. The rest were dressed well, as befitted the day, even Richard, but they did not wear dress coats. Anna was in a gleaming blue silk. It had been bought for her by Isaac, as had a great many other things during their brief period of married life; and poor Mrs. Copp had to invent no end of stories to the captain on their return to Coastdown, saying they were presents from her sick sister. Altogether there were twelve at table.

The housekeeping at the Red Court proved itself just as well prepared for these impromptu guests as it ever had been, save in the one memorable instance marked by the interference of Lady Ellis. After-circumstances caused the items of the bill of fare to be discussed out of doors, and, indeed, every other detail, great and small, of the eventful night. Mock-turtle soup, a fine codfish, a round of beef boiled, a large roast turkey and tongue, side dishes, a plum pudding, sweets, and macaroni. All these were cooked and served in the best manner, with various vegetables, rich and plentiful sauces, strong ale, and the best of wines. Mr. Kyne thought of his solitary tea at home, and licked his lips.

On the withdrawal of the cloth, for Justice Thornycroft preserved that old-fashioned custom, and Mr. Southall had said grace, the young ladies retired. The gentlemen closed round the table to enjoy their wine. A merry party. By and by, spirits, cigars, and pipes were introduced —the usual practice on these occasions at the Red Court. The only one who did not touch them was Cyril Thornycroft.

It had been Mr. Kyne's intention to retire at eight o'clock pre—cisely (he emphasised the word to himself), and go on the watch; or, at any rate, see that his subordinate was there. But the best of officers are but mortal; Mr. Kyne felt very jolly where he was; and, as common sense whispered him, the smuggling lads were safe not to attempt any bother on a Sunday night; they would be jollifying for themselves. So the officer sat on, paying his respects to the brandy-and-water, and getting rather dizzy about the eyes.

Another who stayed longer than he ought; at least, longer than he had intended; was Robert Hunter. Seduced into taking a cigar—and never were such cigars smoked as Justice Thornycroft's—he sat on, and let the time slip by unheeded. On ordinary evenings the omnibus left Coastdown at half-past nine o'clock to convey passengers to the last train, that passed through Jutpoint at midnight. On Sunday nights the omnibus left at half-past eight, some dim notion swaying the minds of the authorities that the earlier hour implied a sort of respect to the day. The convenience of the passengers went for nothing; they had to wait at Jutpoint where and how they could. It had been Robert Hunter's intention to go by this omnibus, and it was only by seeing Isaac Thornycroft look at his watch that he remembered time was flying. He pulled out his own.

"By Jove, I've missed the omnibus," he whispered to Cyril, who sat next him. "It is half-past eight now."

"What shall you do?"

"Walk it. I must be in London for to-morrow morning."

Rising as he spoke, he quietly said farewell to

Mr. Thornycroft, Richard, Isaac, and Mr. Kyne, and stole from the room, not to disturb the other guests, who were seated round the fire now in a cloud of tobacco smoke. Cyril went out with him. Miss Thornycroft and Anna were in the drawing-room drinking coffee. A cup was passed to Robert Hunter.

"What a sad thing—to have to walk to Jutpoint !" exclaimed Mary Anne.

He laughed at the words. "I shall enjoy it far more than I should the omnibus."

"Ah, I think you must have stayed on purpose, then. But what of the portmanteau ?"

"It can come by train to-morrow, if one of your servants will take it to the Mermaid," was his answer. "My address is on it."

As he was speaking, Lady Ellis's maid came into the room and delivered him a small bit of twisted paper. Holding it to the light, he read the faintly-pencilled words.

"I hear you are leaving. Will you come up for a minute, that I may wish you well ?"

"What is it ?" asked Mary Anne.

"Lady Ellis wishes to say farewell to me," he answered. "I will go to her now."

The maid led the way, and showed him up to

the small sitting-room. Lady Ellis was leaning
back in her easy-chair, but she sat upright when
he entered. Even more than before was he
struck with the white, hollow, skeleton look of
the face, on which death had so unmistakably set
his seal; but the disorder had arrived at that
stage now when each day made a perceptible
change. The black eyes, once glistening so
fiercely with their vain passions, lighted up with
a faint pleasure.

"I am glad you came up: so glad! I thought
you did not intend to see me at all."

He answered that he did not know she was
well enough to be seen, speaking cordially. With
that dying face and form before him, three-parts
of his cherished enmity to the woman died out.
Not his dislike of her.

"I would bid you farewell, Mr. Hunter. I
would wish you—an' you will permit me—God-
speed. The next time we meet, both of us will
have entered on a different world from this."

"Thank you," he said, in allusion to the wish,
"but are you sure nothing can be done for your
recovery?"

"Nothing whatever. And the end cannot be
very far off now. Mr. Thornycroft is going back

with me to Cheltenham, and I am glad of it. I should like him to see the last of me."

She was looking at the fire as she spoke. He, standing at the opposite side of the mantelpiece, looked at her. What a change from the vain, worldly, selfish woman of the past! Raising her eyes suddenly, she caught his gaze, perhaps divined somewhat of his thoughts.

" You cannot think me to be the same, can you?"

" Scarcely." He glanced at the timepiece. At best, the interview was not pleasant to him, neither did he care to prolong it.

" You fear to lose the omnibus?"

" I have lost it. Your clock is slow. I am now about to start on foot to Jutpoint."

" Could they not send you in the dogcart?"

" Thank you; I prefer to walk. The night is fine, and the road good. And I suppose I must be going."

She stood up as he moved, and held out her hand, her silk gown falling in folds from her shrunken form. He shook hands.

" God bless you; God prosper you here and hereafter!" she said with some emotion.

He hardly knew what to answer. To express

a wish for her continued life was so palpable a fallacy, with those signs of decay before him : so he murmured a word of thanks, and gave the thin hand a friendly pressure as he released it.

But she did not release his. " It was not quite all I wished to say," she whispered, looking up to him with her sad eyes, in which stood a world of repentance. " I want to ask your forgiveness."

" My forgiveness ?"

" For the past. For your lost wife. But for me she might not have died. My long illness has brought reflection home to me, and—and repentance : as I suppose hopeless illness does to most people : showing me things in their true light ; showing me the awful mistakes and sins the best and the worst of us alike commit. Say that you forgive me."

" Lady Ellis," he said, his countenance assuming a solemn aspect as he looked straight at her, " I have far more need of forgiveness myself than any other can have : I saw that at the time ; I see it always. My wife was mine ; it was my duty to cherish her, and I failed ; no one else owed obligation to her. The chief blame lay with me."

"Say you forgive me! I know *she* has, look-ing down from heaven."

"I do indeed. I forgive you with my whole heart, and I pray that we may, as you say, meet hereafter—all our mistakes and sins blotted out."

"I pray it always. Cyril knows I do. He was the first to lead me—ah, so kindly and im-perceptibly!—to the remembrance that our sins needed blotting out. It was during a six weeks' visit he paid me with his sister. Few in this world are so good and pure and loving as Cyril Thornycroft. Fare you well, Robert Hunter! fare you well for ever."

"For ever on earth," he added. Another pressure of the poor weak hand, a warm, earnest look, a faint thought of the Heaven that might be attained to yet, and Robert Hunter turned away, and woke up to the world again.

His cold coffee stood in the drawing-room when he got back. He sat a short while with the two young ladies, very quiet and absorbed. Cyril was not there. Mary Anne inquired what was the matter with him.

"That poor woman upstairs," he briefly an-swered; "she seems so near to death, but I think she is prepared for it."

Mary Anne Thornycroft simply looked at him in reply; the manner and look were alike strange. Robert Hunter sipped the cold coffee by spoonfuls, evidently unconscious what it was he was doing.

"But I must be going!" he suddenly cried, starting up. "It would not do to miss the train as I have the omnibus. Good-bye, Anna; you will be coming back to Miss Jupps's, I suppose, when school begins?"

The vivid blush went for nothing. She, Mrs. Isaac Thornycroft, a school-teacher again! "Good-bye, Robert," she softly said. "I wish you safe to Jutpoint, but I should not like your walk. Give my love to the Miss Jupps if you see them, and to Mrs. Macpherson."

Mary Anne went out with him to the door. As they crossed the hall, sounds of talking came from the dining-room, and there was a sudden burst of laughter. Evidently the party were enjoying themselves. He took his remarkable coat from a peg and flung it over his arm.

"You must say good-bye to Cyril for me, Mary Anne."

"I will. But perhaps you will see him outside. Why don't you put your coat on?"

"Not yet; I am hot. By-and-by, when the air shall strike cool to me."

They stood just outside the door, in the shade of the walls, and he wound his arms round her for a last embrace. *A last?* "God bless you, Mary Anne!" he whispered; "the time will come, I trust, when we need not part."

She stood looking after him, the outline of his retreating form being very distinct in the bright night. The stars were clear and the air was frosty. Mary Anne Thornycroft watched him pass through the gate, and then saw that instead of going straight on, he turned short off to the waste land skirting the side of the plateau.

She wondered. It was the farthest way to the village, and moreover the private way of Mr. Thornycroft. Another moment and she saw him running up the plateau, having crossed the railings.

"Why, what in the world!—he must be dreaming," she mentally concluded. "Perhaps he wants to take a farewell view of the sea. He would see enough of it between here and Jut-point."

However, Miss Thornycroft found it cold standing there, and went indoors, meeting Sinnett in the hall.

" Sinnett, Mr. Hunter's portmanteau must go by the early omnibus. See that it is sent to the Mermaid in time."

" Very well, miss," replied Sinnett. And it may be here mentioned that she obeyed the order by sending it that night.

Very shortly after Robert Hunter had left the dining-room, Richard and Isaac Thornycroft also withdrew from it, one by one, and unperceived. That is, the guests and the justice were too agreeably engaged with their pipes and drink, their talk and laughter, to pay heed to it. One of the gentlemen from Jutpoint—a magistrate— was relating a story that convulsed the parson with laughter and sent the rest almost into fits. Altogether they were uncommonly jolly, and the lapse of one or two of the party counted for nothing. Mr. Kyne had nearly ceased to care whether his subordinate was on the watch, or off it.

As it happened, he was *on* it. With the promised visit of his superior before his eyes, Mr. Puffer had not dared to leave his post. He stood close to the bleak edge of the cold plateau,

wishing himself anywhere else, and bemoaning
the hard fate that had made him a coastguards-
man. Unpleasant thoughts of ghosts, and such
like visitants, intruded into his thoughts now and
then : he entirely disbelieved Mr. Kyne's theory
that there were smugglers; and the only cheer-
ing ray in his solitude, was the sight of the cheery
lights in the Red Court Farm. Tomlett, the
fishing-boat master, who had recovered his accident, suddenly hailed him.

"Cold work, my man," said he, sauntering up
the plateau.

"It just is that!" was Mr. Puffer's surly
answer.

"But it's a bright night : never saw a brighter
when there was no moon : so you run no danger
of making a false step in the dark and pitching
over. There's consolation in that."

"Ugh !" grunted the shivering officer, as if
the fact afforded little consolation to him.

"What on earth's the use of your airing yourself here?" went on Tomlett. "You coastguard fellows have got the biggest swallows ! As
if any smugglers would attempt the coast to-night !
My belief is—and I am pretty well used to the
place, and have got eyes on all sides of me—

that this suspicion of Master Kyne's is all moon-
shine and empty herring-barrels. I could nearly
take my oath of it."

" So could I," said the man.

" Let us go on to the Mermaid, and have a
glass," continued Mr. Tomlett, persuasively. " I'll
stand it. Johnson and Simms, and a lot more,
are there."

" I wish I dare," cried the aggravated Puffer.
" But Kyne will be up presently."

" No he won't. He is round old Thorny-
croft's fire, in a cloud of smoke and drink.
There's a dinner-party at the Red Court, and
Kyne and the rest are half-seas over."

" Are you sure of this ?"

" I'll swear it if you wish me; I have just
come from there. I went down to try and get
speech of the justice about that boat loss : it
comes on at Jutpoint to-morrow, and he is to be
on the bench. But it was no go: they are all
fixed in that dining-room; and will be there till
twelve o'clock to-night, and then they'll reel off
to bed with their boots on."

Tomlett was not in the habit of deceiving the
men ; he showed himself their friend on all
occasions; and Mr. Puffer yielded to the se-

duction. Seeing him comfortably settled at the Mermaid, with what he liked best steaming before him, and some good fellows around, Tomlett withdrew, leaving him to enjoy himself.

From the Mermaid, Tomlett steered his course to the Red Court Farm, tearing over the intervening ground as if he had been flying from a mad bull. He took the liberty of crossing the lawn before the front windows (the shortest way), and went round by the unused path at the far end of the house, which led to the stables and to the young men's apartments. Carefully pushing open the small door in the dead wall, he encountered Richard Thornycroft.

"It is all right, sir," he panted, out of breath with running; "I have got the fellow in. We must lose no time."

"Very well," whispered Richard. "Find Hyde, and come down."

"I suppose *he's* safe, sir?" said Mr. Tomlett, jerking his head in the supposed direction of the dining-room.

"Couldn't be safer," responded Richard. "He had enough wine before he began at the brandy."

Isaac Thornycroft came up, a lighted lantern under his coat. Scarcely could either of the

brothers be recognised for those who had so recently quitted the dining-room; they wore small
caps; gaiters were buttoned over their legs; their
dinner coats were replaced by coarse ones of
fustian.

CHAPTER II.

WHEN Richard and Isaac Thornycroft left the dining-room, so unobtrusively as not to draw attention to the fact, they passed through the small door at the further end of the hall. Isaac, the last, silently locked it, thereby cutting off all communication with the busy part of the house. Swiftly ascending to Richard's chamber, they changed their clothes for others which were laid out in readiness. Hyde, his clothes also changed, was in waiting at the foot of the stairs when they came down, and he crossed with Isaac to the coach-house opposite, built, as must be remembered, on a portion of the old ruins. Richard undid the door in the wall looking to the front, and stayed there until joined by the breathless Tomlett—as above seen.

The dog-cart was in its place in the coach-house; the broken old cart and the bundles of

straw were in the corner; all just as usual.
Tomlett and Hyde removed the cart and the
straw from their resting place (whence, by all
appearance, they never were removed), and the
brothers Thornycroft lifted a trap-door, invisible
to the casual observer, that the straw had served to
conceal. A flight of steps stood disclosed to view,
which Isaac and Richard descended. The steps
led to a subterranean passage ; a long, long passage
running straight under the plateau and termina-
ting in a vault or cavern, its damp sides glistening as the light of the lantern flashed upon it.
Traversing this passage to the end, Isaac put the
lantern down : then they unwound a chain from
its pulley, and a square portion of the rock, loose
from the rest, was *pulled in* and turned aside by
means of a pivot : thus affording an ingress for
goods, smuggled or otherwise, to come in. No
wonder Robert Hunter had thought the rock
sounded hollow just there !

Ah, Mr. Kyne had scented the fox pretty keenly.
But not the huntsmen who rode him to earth.

It took longer to do all this than it has to
relate it. When Richard had helped Isaac to
remove the rock, he returned along the passage
on his way to the plateau. It was customary for

one of the two brothers to stand on the plateau on the watch during these dangerous feats, with his descending signal of warning in case of alarm. Richard took that post to-night. Oh, that it had been Isaac! But it was marvellous how lucky they had hitherto been. Years had gone on, and years, and never a check had come. One great reason for this was that the late supervisor, Mr. Dangerfield—let us only whisper it!—had allowed himself to be bribed. What with that, and what with the horror the preventive men had of the plateau, the daring and profitable game had been carried on with impunity. Richard Thornycroft went on his way, little knowing the awful phantom that was pursuing him.

Midway in the passage he met Hyde and Tomlett, tried and true men, on their way to join Isaac. Mr. Tomlett's accident had occurred during one of these night exploits—hence his wife's terrified consternation at being questioned by Miss Thornycroft. A strange chance had led, some years ago, to Mrs. Tomlett's discovery of what her husband was engaged in at intervals: the woman kept the secret, but never was free from fear.

Isaac Thornycroft, left alone, proceeded with
his necessary movements. By help of a long
pole, thrust through the hole, he held forth a
blazing flambeau, which for two minutes would
light up the half-moon beach and the rocks
behind it. It was the signal for the boats to put
off from that especial vessel that was the object
of the worthy supervisor's abhorrence. And so
the night's secret work was fairly inaugurated.
Isaac Thornycroft held his signal for the approach of the boats, laden with their heavy
spoil; Richard was speeding back to assume his
watch overhead; and it was just about this time
that Mr. Hunter had taken his departure from
the Red Court Farm.

It is quite useless to speculate, now, *why*
Robert Hunter went on the plateau. Some
power must have impelled him. These things,
bearing great events in their train, do not occur
by chance. Had he been questioned why, he
probably could not have told. The most likely
conjecture is, speaking according to human
reason, that he intended to stand a few moments
on its brow, and sniff the fresh breeze from the
sea, so grateful to his heated senses. He had
taken more wine than usual; certainly not to

anything like intoxication, for he was by habit
and principle a sober man.   He had dined more
freely; the hot room, the talking, all had contributed to heat him ; and, following on it, came
the interview with Lady Ellis.   Whatever the
cause, certain it is that, instead of pursuing the
straight course of his road, like a sensible man,
he turned off it and went on the plateau.

It was a remarkably light night—as already
said—clear, still, frosty, very bright.   The clouds,
passing occasionally over the face of the clear sky,
seemed to be moved by an upper current that
did not stir the air below.   The sea was like
silver ; no craft to be seen on it save one vessel
that was hove-to close in-shore—a dark vessel,
lying still and silent.   Robert Hunter, at the
very edge of the plateau, stood looking on all
this : a peaceful scene ; the broad expanse of sea
stretching out, the half-moon beach lying cold
and solitary below.

Suddenly a bright sheet of light shot out
from underneath, illumining the half-moon,
the rocks, and his own face, as he bent over to
look.   Was he dreaming ? — was his brain
treacherous, causing him to see things that were
not ?   There, half-way down the rocks, shone a

great flame, a flickering, flaring, blazing flame, as of a torch ; and Robert Hunter rubbed his eyes, and slapped his chest, and pinched his arms, to make sure he was *not* in a dream of wine.

He stood staring at it, his eyes and mouth open ; stared at it until, by some mysterious process, it steadily lowered itself, and disappeared inside the rocks. Light—not of the torch—flashed upon him.

" The smugglers !" he burst forth : and the clear night air carried the words over the sea. " The smugglers are abroad to-night ! That must be their signal for the booty to approach. Then there *is* an opening in the rocks ! I'll hasten and give word to Kyne."

Flying back straight towards the Red Court, he had leaped the railings when he encountered Richard Thornycroft, who seemed to be flying along with equal speed towards the plateau. Hunter seized his arm.

" Richard Thornycroft ! Mr. Richard ! the smugglers are at work ! I have dropped upon them. Their signal has been hoisted beyond the rocks underneath."

" What ?" roared Richard.

" It is true as that we are breathing here,"

continued Hunter. " I went on the plateau, and I saw their light—a flaming torch as big as your head. They are preparing to run the goods. It struck me there must be an opening there. I am going to fetch Kyne. Mr. Thornycroft, if he will come out, may be convinced now."

He would have resumed his way with the last words, but Richard caught him. The slight form of Robert Hunter was whirled round in his powerful grasp.

" Do you see this ?" he hoarsely raved, his face wearing an awfully livid expression, born of anger, in the starlight. " It is well loaded."

Robert Hunter did see it. It was the bright end of a pistol barrel, pointed close to his head. He recoiled, as far as he could, but the grasp was tight upon him.

" What, in Heaven's name, do you mean ?"

" *You* talk of Heaven, you treacherous cur !" panted Richard. " Down upon your knees— down, I say ! You shall talk of it to some purpose."

By his superior strength, he forced the younger and slighter man to his knees on the waste ground as he would a child. The fur coat fell from Robert Hunter's arm, and lay beside him, a white heap streaked with black, in the star-light.

" Now, then! Swear, by all your hopes of Heaven, that what you have detected shall never pass your lips ; shall be as if you had not seen it."

" I swear," answered Robert Hunter. " I believe I guess how it is. I will be silent ; I swear it."

" Now and hereafter ?"

" Now and hereafter."

" Get up, then, and go your way. But, another word, first of all," interrupted Richard, as if a thought struck him. " This must be kept secret from my sister."

" I swear that it shall be, for me."

Holding Robert Hunter still in his fierce grasp, he dictated to him yet another oath, as if not satisfied with the last one. In cooler moments neither of them might have acted as they were doing : Richard had been less imperative, the other less blindly yielding. Robert Hunter was no coward, but circumstances and Richard's fury momentarily over-mastered him.

He swore a solemn oath—Richard dictating it —not to hold further communication with Mary

Anne at present, either by word or letter; not to do it until Richard should of his own will voluntarily give permission for it. He swore not again to put foot within the Red Court Farm; he swore not to write to any one of its inmates, failing this permission. The determination not to be pestered with letters perhaps caused Richard to insist on this. Any way, the oaths were taken, and were to hold force for six months.

"Now, then, go your way," said Richard. "Your path for departure lies *there*," and he pointed to the open highway leading from the entrance gates of the Red Court. "But first hear *me* swear an oath that I shall surely keep: If you do not go straight away; if you linger on this spot unnecessarily by so much as a few minutes; if you, having once started, return to it again, I will put this bullet through your body. Cyril! See him off; he was turning traitor."

Cyril Thornycroft had come strolling towards them, somewhat at a distance yet; he did not catch the sense of his brother's concluding words, but he saw that some explosion of anger had occurred. Picking up the coat, Hunter put it on as he walked to join Cyril; while Richard, as if under the pressure of some urgent errand, flew off across the lawn and flower-beds towards the coach-house ruins and the secret passage leading from it.

" What is all this? What does Richard mean?" inquired Cyril as they commenced their walk along the high road. " He said something about a traitor."

" I was not a traitor; your brother lies. Would I turn traitor to a house whose hospitality I have been accepting? I saw, accidentally, a light exhibited from the Half-moon rocks, and I guessed what it meant. I guess more now than I will repeat, but the secret shall be safe with me."

" Safe now, and after your departure?"

" Safe always. I have sworn it."

" I am sorry this should have happened," said Cyril, after a pause.

" And so am I," returned Robert Hunter. " Circumstances, not my own will, led to it. It is a pity I missed the omnibus."

" Yes," said Cyril, speaking abstractedly, as if his thoughts were far away. " But if you step out well you may be at Jutpoint by half-past ten."

" Scarcely so," thought Robert Hunter. Cyril, perhaps, did not know the hour now.

"What! Have you missed the omnibus, sir?"

The question came from a woman who met them, Captain Copp's servant Sarah. She was coming along without her bonnet in the frosty night.

"Yes, I have; and must walk it for my pains," answered Mr. Hunter.

"Are you going to the Red Court, Sarah?" asked Cyril.

"I am, sir; I'm going there to fetch Miss Chester," returned Sarah in her hardest tone. "And a fine tantrum master's in over it, roaring out that I ought to have come a good hour ago. Why didn't they tell me, then?"

Saying good night to the woman, who wished Mr. Hunter a pleasant journey, they continued their way, striking into the village; a silent village to-night. In the windows of the Mermaid above, lights were no doubt gleaming, but they were not near enough to that hospitable hostelry to see. Everybody else seemed abed and asleep, as was generally the case at Coastdown by nine o'clock on a Sunday night.

Cyril had fallen into thought. Should he offer Hunter any apology or excuse for these practices of his house, so inopportunely disco-

vered, and which had always been so distasteful
to him ? Better not, perhaps. What excusing
plea could he justly offer? And besides, he
knew not how far the discovery went, or what
Richard had said. A feeling of resentment
against Robert Hunter rose up in his heart, in
his anxiety to ward off ill from his father and
brothers, in his jealous care for the fair fame of
the Red Court Farm. Good though he was,
striving ever to follow in his Master's footsteps of
love and peace, Cyril Thornycroft was but human,
with a human heart disposed by its original
nature to passion and sin.

"Let me advise you, at any rate for the present, not to hold communication with our
house or its inmates," he said, gently breaking
the silence. "In this I include my sister."

"I have promised all that. Your brother was
not satisfied with exacting a simple promise ; he
made me swear it. I was to have written to Mary
Anne on my arrival in town. Will you explain
to her the reason why I do not?"

"I thought you and my sister did not correspond," interrupted Cyril.

"Neither do we. It was only to notify my
safe arrival."

" I will explain sufficient to satisfy her. I
suppose I must not ask you to give her
up ?"

" My intention is to win her if I can," avowed
Robert Hunter.   " She would share my fortunes
to-morrow, but for the fear that my position
would not be acceptable to Mr. Thornycroft."

" I see ; it is decided.   Well, in your own
interest, I would advise you to break off all present relations with our house.   What has occurred
to-night will not tend to increase Richard's favour
to you, and his opinion very greatly sways my
father.   Your visit here, taking it on the whole,
has not been pleasant, or productive of pleasant
results.   Give us time to forget it and you *for
the present*.   Give Richard time to forget the
name and sojourn of Robert Hunter."

" You say you suggest this in my own interest ?"

" I do indeed," answered Cyril, his good,
calm face turning on the speaker with a kindly
light.   " In yours and my sister's jointly.   She
will be true to you, I make no doubt ; and things
may come about after a short while.   If you
have decided to take each other, if your best
affections are involved, why should I seek to part

you? But I know what Richard is; you must give him time to get over this."

"True," answered Robert Hunter, his heart responding to the evident kindness. "At any rate, there can be no question of my holding communication with the Red Court Farm for six months, even by letter. It was a rash oath, no doubt; I was not quite myself when I took it; but I have undertaken not to write to any one of you until Richard shall give me leave. At the end of the six months I suppose I shall hear from him; if not, I shall consider myself at liberty to write—or to come."

" You will surely hear from him if he has implied that you shall. Richard never breaks a promise. And now that I have seen you thus far on your way, I'll wish you well, and turn back again."

" They had reached the end of the village, and he grasped Robert Hunter's hand with a warm and friendly pressure. The other was loth to part with him so soon.

" You may as well go with me as far as the Wherry."

Robert Hunter spoke not of a boat or of any landing for one, but of a lone and dismantled public

house, standing about a couple of hundred yards
farther. Its sign swung on it still, and rattled
in the wind. Cyril acquiesced, and they went
down into the bit of lonely road leading to it.

We must go back for a moment to Richard
Thornycroft. He gained the ruins, and lifted
the trap-door with, as it seemed, almost super-
human strength, for it took of right two to do it.
Completely upset by what had occurred, Richard
was like a man half mad. He went thundering
down the steps to the subterranean passage, his
errand being to give warning to Isaac, and assist
in hoisting *two* lights, which those on board the
vessel would understand as the signal *not* to advance. He had reached the cavern at the end,
when his alarm began to subside, to give place to
reason ; and his steps came to a sudden stand-
still.

" Why stop the boats ?" he demanded of himself. " If Hunter has cleared himself off—of
which there can be no doubt — where is the
danger ?"

Where, indeed ? He thought—Richard Thornycroft did think—that Hunter was not one to play
false after undertaking to be true. So, after a
little more deliberation, somewhat further of

counsel with himself, he resolved to let things go
on, and turned back again without warning Isaac.

*   *   *   *   *

What mattered it that the contraband cargo
was safely run ? What recked the guilty parties
concerned in it of the miserable deed of evil it
involved, while the valuable and double valuable
booty got stowed away in silence and safety ?
One was lying outside the Half-moon, while they
housed it, with his battered face turned up to the
sky—one whose departed soul had been worth all
the cargoes in the world. The body was bruised,
and crushed, and *murdered*—the body of Robert
Hunter !

How did it come there ?

*   *   *   *   *

Coastdown woke lazily up from its slumbers
with the dawn—not very early in January—and
only got roused into life and activity by the
startling piece of news that a shocking murder
had been committed in the night. Hastening
down to its alleged scene, the Half-moon beach,
as many as heard it, shopkeepers, fishermen, and
inhabitants generally, they found it to be too true.
The poor man lay in the extreme corner of the
strip of beach, right against the rocks, and was

recognised for the late guest at the Red Court Farm, Robert Hunter.

Not by his face; for that was disfigured beyond possibility of recognition; but by the clothes, hair, and appearance generally. He had been shot in the face, and, in falling from the heights above, the jagged edges of the rocks had also disfigured that poor face until not a trace of its humanity remained.

The tide was low; at present the passage to the beach was passable, and stragglers were flocking up. The frosty air was crisp, the sea sparkled in the early morning sun. Amidst others came Justice Thornycroft, upright, portly, a smile on his handsome face. He did not believe the report; as was evident by his greeting words.

"What's all this hullabaloo about a murder?" began he, as he shelved round the narrow ledge and put his foot upon the beach. "How d'ye do, Kyne?—How d'ye do, Copp—How d'ye do, all? When Martha brought up my shaving-water just now, she burst into my room, her hair and mouth all awry with a story of a man having been murdered in the night at the Half-moon. Some poor drowned fellow, I suppose,

cast on the banks by the tide. What brings
him so high up?"

"I wish it was drowning, and nothing worse,
for that's not such an uncivilized death, if it's
your fate to meet it," returned Captain Copp,
who was brisk this morning after his headache,
and had stumped down on the first alarm. "It's
a horrible land murder; nothing less; and upon
a friend of yours, justice."

"A friend of mine!" was the somewhat in-
credulous remark of Mr. Thornycroft. "Why,
good Heaven!" he added, in an accent of horror,
as the crowd parted and he caught sight of the
body, "it is my late guest, Robert Hunter!"

"It is indeed," murmured the crowd; and the
justice stood gazing at it with horror as he took
in the different points of recognition. The face
was gone—that is the best term for one so utterly
unrecognisable—but the appearance and dress
were not to be mistaken.

"He's buttoned close up in his fur coat, sir,"
one of the crowd remarked.

Just so. He was buttoned up in his remarkable fur coat—as the village wrongly called it, for
the coat was of white cloth, as we know, and its
facings only of fur. It had stains on it now,

neither white nor black, and one of its sleeves
was torn, no doubt by the rocks. The hat was
nowhere to be found : it never was found : but
the natural supposition was, that in the fall it
had rolled down to the lower beach, and been
carried away by the tide.

Mr. Thornycroft stooped, and touched one of
the cold hands, stooped to hide the tears which
filled his eyes, very unusual visitors to the eyes of
the justice.

" Poor, poor fellow ! how could it have happened ?   How could he have come here ?"

" He must have been shot on the heights,
and the shot hurled him over, there's no doubt
of that," said Captain Copp.   " Must have been
standing at the edge of the plateau."

" But what should bring him on the plateau
at night?" cried Tomlett, who made one of the
spectators.

" What indeed !" returned the captain.   " *I*
don't know.   A bare, bleak place even in daylight, with as good as no expanse of sea-view."

" I cannot understand this," said Justice
Thornycroft, lifting his face with a puzzled expression on it.   " Young Hunter took leave of us
last night, and left for London.   He missed the

omnibus to Jutpoint and set off to walk. One of my sons saw him part of the way. What brought him back on the plateau ?"

" Yes, he contrived to lose the omnibus," interrupted Supervisor Kyne ; who, however, what with the wine and the brandy he had consumed, had a very confused and imperfect recollection of the events of the previous evening, but did not choose to let people know that, and chose to put in his testimony. " Mr. Hunter shook hands with me in the dining-room at the Red Court, and I wished him a pleasant journey. That must have been—what time, Mr. Justice ?"

" Getting on for nine. And one of my boys saw him go."

" It's odd what could have spirited him back again," exclaimed Captain Copp. " Which of them steered him off ?"

" I forget which," returned the justice. " I heard Isaac say that one of them did. To tell you the truth, captain, I sat late in the dining-room last night, and my head's none of the clearest this morning. How do you find yours, Kyne ?"

" Oh, mine's all right, sir," answered the

supervisor hastily. "A man in office is obliged to be cautious in what he takes."

"Ah, there's no coming over you," cried the justice, with a side wink to Captain Copp.

"There's Mr. Isaac hisself, a coming round the point now," exclaimed one of the fishermen.

The crowd turned and saw him. Isaac Thornycroft was approaching with a rapid step.

"They say Hunter is murdered!" he called out. "It cannot be."

"He is lying here, stiff and cold, Isaac, with a bullet in his head," was the sad reply of the justice. "Shot down from the heights above."

Isaac stooped in silence. His fair complexion and fine colour, heightened by the morning air, were something bright to look upon. But, as he gazed at that sadly disfigured form, yesterday so animate with life and health, a paleness as of the grave overspread his face; a shudder, which shook him from head to foot, passed through his frame.

"What brought him here—or on the plateau?" he asked. Almost the same words his father had used.

"What indeed!" repeated Mr. Thornycroft.

" Did you tell me you saw him off, Isaac ?   Or
was it Richard ?"

" It was Cyril.   I did not see him at all after
he wished us good-bye on leaving the dining-
room.   But Richard, when he joined me later
in the evening, said he had been—had been,"
repeated Isaac, having rather hesitated at these
words, " saying a parting word to Hunter, and
that Cyril was walking part of the way with
him."

Throwing a pocket handkerchief lightly over
the disfigured face, Isaac Thornycroft turned
from it towards the sea.   The justice spoke.

" I wonder where Cyril left him ?"

To wonder it was only natural, but Mr.
Thornycroft's remembrances of the matter, as to
what he had heard, were altogether hazy.   Shut
up so long in the dining-room with his guests—
for they had not parted until past midnight—
doing his part as host at the pipes and grog,
though not very extensively, for it was rare
indeed that Mr. Thornycroft took too much, he
was in a tired, sleepy state when Isaac had come
to him after their departure to say that the work
was done, the cargo safely in.   Isaac had added
that he understood from Richard there had been

some trouble with Hunter; who had seen the torch-light exhibited on the Half-moon beach, and Richard had been obliged to swear him to secrecy, and had sent Cyril to see him safe away. Of all this, the justice retained an indistinct remembrance.

"Yes," he said slowly, "I recollect now; it was Cyril that you said, Isaac. We must go and find Cyril, and ascertain where he parted with Hunter."

"Why!" suddenly exclaimed a young fisherman of the name of East, "I saw them both together last night; the gentleman and Mr. Cyril. I'd been down at my old mother's and was coming out to go home, when they passed, a walking in the middle of the road. I'd never have noticed 'em, may be, but for the fur coat, for they'd got some way ahead. I see them stop and stand together like, and shake hands as if they was about to part; and then they went on again."

"Both of them went on again?" questioned Isaac.

"Yes, sir, both. They went on into the hollow, and I came away."

This young man's mother lived in a solitary

hut at the end of the village : in fact, just where Cyril had proposed to leave Hunter, and East must have come out at the same moment.

" We'll go at once and see what Cyril says," resumed the justice, moving away.   " Hunter must have come back with him."

" What is to be done with Mr. Hunter, sir ?" questioned Tomlett, who had some sort of authority in the place.   It did seem like a mockery to call that poor mass of death lying there " Mr. Hunter."

He must be taken to the Mermaid, was the reply of Justice Thornycroft, as he left the beach with his son and three or four friends.   " You had better come up and see Pettipher : he'll know what's right to be done.   Don't be all the morning about it, Tomlett, or you will have the tide over the path."

Anything for more excitement in a moment like the present !   Tomlett, following closely on the steps of Justice Thornycroft, went away with a fleet foot on his errand to the Mermaid, and the whole lot of hearers went racing after him : leaving Captain Copp, who could not race, and Mr. Supervisor Kyne to keep guard over the dead.   Her Majesty's officer might have

4—2

gone with the rest, but that he was in a brown study.

"There's more in this than meets the eye, captain," he began, rousing himself. " If this has not been the work of smugglers, my name's not John Kyne."

" Smugglers be shivered!" returned Captain Copp, who it was pretty well suspected in the village obtained his spirits and tobacco without any trouble to her majesty's revenue : as did others. " There are no smugglers here, Mr. Officer. And if there were, what should they want with murdering Robert Hunter ?"

" I have been on the work and watch for weeks, captain, and I know there *is* smuggling carried on ; and to a deuced pretty extent."

" We are rich enough to buy our own brandy and pay duty on it, Mr. Supervisor," wrathfully retorted the offended captain.

" Oh, psha ! I am not looking after the paltry dabs of brandy they bring ashore," returned the customs' officer. One may as well try to wash a blackamoor white as to stop that. I look after booty of more consequence. There are cargoes of dry goods run here ; foreign lace at a guinea a yard."

"My eye!" ejaculated Captain Copp in amazement, who was willing enough to hear the suspicions, now he found they did not point to anything likely to affect his comfort. "Where do they run them to?"

"They run them here, as I believe; here on the Half-moon; and I suspect they must have a hiding-place somewhere in these rocks."

To describe the intense wonder depicted on the face of the ex-merchant captain would be impossible. It ended in a laugh of incredulity, anything but flattering to his hearer.

"I could swear it," persisted the supervisor, "There! Only a few days ago, I was telling my suspicions to this poor fellow"—glancing over his shoulder—"and he offered to help me ferret out the matter. He came down with me here, examined the rocks, sounded them (he was an engineer, as perhaps you know), and appointed a further hunt for the next day. I never saw a man more interested, or more eager to pounce on the offenders. But before the next day arrived I happened to meet him, and he said he must apologize for not keeping his promise, but he preferred not to interfere further. When I pressed him for his reason he only hemmed and ha-ed, and said that, being a stranger, the neighbourhood might deem his doing so an impertinence. Which of course was sheer rubbish."

Captain Copp, rather slow at taking in ideas, began considering what his own opinion was. The supervisor went on, his tone impressive.

" Now, captain, it is my firm belief that this sudden change and Mr. Hunter's constrained manner, were caused by his having received some private hint from the smugglers themselves not to aid me in my search; and that it is nobody but they who have put it out of his power to do so."

" Whew !" whistled the staggered captain. " I could make more of a sinking ship than of what you say. Who are the smugglers ? How did they find out he was going to interfere—unless he or you sent 'em word ?"

" I don't know how they found it out. The affair is a mystery from beginning to end. Nobody was present at the conversation except Miss Thornycroft. And she cannot be suspected of holding communication with smugglers."

" This young fellow was a sweetheart of hers —eh ?" cried the shrewd captain.

" I don't know anything about that. They

seemed intimate. I could almost swear Old Nick
has to do with this smuggling business," added
the supervisor, earnestly. " A fortnight ago there
was a dinner at the Red Court—you were there,
by-the-way."

" A jolly spread the old justice gave us!
Prime drink and cigars," chimed in the salt
tar.

" Well—I was there : and one can't be in two
places at once. That very evening they managed
to run their cargo ; ran it on, as I suspect, to
this identical spot, sir," cried the disconcerted
officer, warming with his grievance. " Vexed
enough I was, and never once have I been off
the watch since. Every night have I took up
my station on that cursed damp plateau overhead, my stomach stretched on the ground, to
keep myself dark, and just half an eye cocked
out over the cliff—and all to no purpose. Last
night, Sunday, I went in again to dine with the
hospitable justice, and I'll be—I'll be shivered,
sir, as you sometimes say, if they did not take
advantage of it, and run another cargo !"

Never, since the memorable time of his
encounter with the pirates which resulted in
the disabling him for life, had Captain Copp

been so struck—dumb, as it were. Nothing was left of him but amazement.

"Bless and save my wooden leg!" he exclaimed, when his tongue was found—"it is unbelievable. How do you know it?"

"I know it, and that's enough," replied Mr. Kyne, too much annoyed to stand upon politeness, or to explain that his boasted knowledge was assumed; not proved. "But, here's the devil of the thing," he continued—"how did the smugglers know I was off the watch those two particular nights? If it got wind the first night that I should be engaged at the Red Court—though I don't believe it did, for I can keep my own counsel, and did then—it could not have got wind the second. Five minutes before I went there last night, I had no notion whatever of going. Mr. Isaac looked into my rooms just before six, and *would* walk me off with him. I had had my chop at one o'clock, and was going to think about tea. Now how could the wretches have known last night that I was not on duty?"

"It's no good appealing to me, how," returned the captain. "I never was 'cute at breaking up marvels. Once, in the Pacific, there was a great

big thing haunted the ship, bigger than the biggest sea-serpent, and——"

"Depend upon it we have traitors in the
camp," unceremoniously interrupted the supervisor; for he knew by experience that when once
Captain Copp was fairly launched upon that old
marvel of the Pacific ocean, there was no stopping him. "Traitors round about us, at our very
elbows and hearths, if we only knew in which
direction to look for them."

"Well, I am not one," said the captain, "so
you need not look after me. A pretty figure my
wooden standard would cut, running smuggled
goods! Why didn't you tell all this to Justice
Thornycroft? He's the proper person. He's a
magistrate."

"I know he is. But if I introduce a word
about smugglers he throws cold water on it directly, and ridicules all I say. Once he quite
rose up against me, all his bristles on end, in de-
fence of the poor fishermen. Upon that, I
hinted that I was not alluding to poor fishermen,
but to people and transactions of far greater im-
portance. It stirred up his anger beyond everything; he was barely civil, and turned away
telling me to *find* the people and catch 'em,

if I could find 'em; but not to apply to him."

" Well, that's reasonable," said Captain Copp. " Why *don't* you find 'em ?"

" Because I *can't* find 'em," deplored the miserable officer. " There's the aggravation. I don't know in what quarter to look for them. The thing is like magic; it's altogether shrouded in mystery. I don't choose to speak of it publicly, or I might defeat the chance of discovery; the only time I did speak of it, was to Mr. Hunter, and got sympathy and aid offered and returned to me. You see what has come of that."

It was only too evident what *he* thought had come of it. And perhaps he was not far wrong. But for that recent morning's unlucky conversation between him and Robert Hunter, no dead man might have been lying on the Half-moon beach, with Isaac Thornycroft's handkerchief covering his face.

" Yes, that's the difficulty—where to look for them," resumed the mortified supervisor. "I cannot suspect any of the superior people in the neighbourhood. It's true I do not know much of those Connaughts. But they don't seem like smugglers either."

" The Connaughts !" roared out the captain, taking up their cause as a personal offence. "Why don't you say it's me? Why don't you say it's yourself? The Connaughts ! Who next, Mr. Supervisor? Why, old Connaught is bedridden half his time, and the son has got his eyes strained on books all day, learning to be a parson."

" That's true," grumbled the officer, in his miserable incertitude. " All I know is, I can't fathom the affair, worry over it as I will."

" Here comes the plank," interrupted the captain. " I shan't stop to see *that* moved : so good morning to you, sir."

He stumped off, mortally offended ; and met Tomlett and the landlord of the Mermaid inn, with the long queue of curious idlers behind them.

CHAPTER III.

SHOT DOWN FROM THE HEIGHTS.

In the breakfast-room at the Red Court Farm, seated at its well-laid morning-table, was Richard Thornycroft. Seated at it only: not eating: his plate was unsupplied, his coffee stood cold before him. He seemed to be in some unpleasant meditation, every line of his dark face speaking of perplexity.

To be broken in upon by the irruption of numerous visitors, evidently astonished him not a little. The attendants on Mr. Thornycroft had gathered on the way from the Half-moon beach, just as some balls gather in rolling, and six or seven friends followed in on the tail of the master of the Red Court Farm. Isaac, on the contrary, seemed to have fallen away from it, for he did not enter with the rest. Richard rose to welcome them, with scant courtesy.

" Where's Cyril?" began the justice. " Is
he down yet?"

" I don't know," answered Richard, taking
out his watch and glancing at it. " I have not
seen him. It is early yet."

" And Cyril never is very early," added the
justice, quickly assuming that his youngest son
was in his bed still. " Have you heard the news,
Richard?"

" Yes," was Richard's laconic answer.

" What do you think of it? How do you
suppose it could have happened?"

" I don't think about it," returned Richard.
" I conclude that if he did not shoot himself, he
must have got into some quarrelling fray. He
drank enough wine last evening to heat his
brain, and we had proof that he was fond of
meddling in what did not concern him. The
extraordinary part of the business is, what
brought him back on the plateau, after he had
once started on his journey."

" I'll go up and arouse Cyril, and know where
he left Hunter. Gentlemen, if you will sit down
and take some breakfast, we shall be glad of
your company. There's a capital round of beef.
Hallo, you girls!" called out the justice, striding

away in the direction of the kitchen, "some of you come in here and attend. Sinnett, let some more ham and eggs be sent in."

Nothing loath, the gentlemen responded at once to the invitation : most of them had not breakfasted. The Rev. Mr. Southall made one. The round of beef was capital, as its master said ; the game pies looked tempting, the cold ham, the hot rolls, the fresh eggs, the toasted bacon, all were excellent. Apparently, the Red Court Farm kept itself prepared for an impromptu public breakfast, just as well as it did for an impromptu dinner.

Mr. Thornycroft ascended the stairs, and presently his voice was heard on the landing, calling to Cyril. But it died away in the echoes of the large house, and there was no answer; unless the opening of the door of his wife's room by her maid could be called such.

"Did you want anything, sir?" she asked, looking out.

"Nothing particular. How is your lady this morning ?"

"Much the same, sir, thank you."

The maid shut the door again, and Mr. Thornycroft went on to Cyril's chamber. He found it empty. It was so unusual for Cyril to be up and out early, that he felt a sort of surprise. That he had not gone far, however, was evident, as his watch and purse lay on the chest of drawers. The justice crossed the corridor and knocked at his daughter's room.

"Are you up, Mary Anne?"

"Yes," responded a faint and hurried voice within. "What do you want, papa?"

"I want you. Open the door."

But Miss Thornycroft did not obey. The justice, never remarkable for patience, when his behests were disregarded, laid hold of the handle and shook it with his strong hand.

"Open the door, I say, Mary Anne. What, girl! are you afraid of me?"

Miss Thornycroft slowly opened the door, and presented herself. She was in a handsome grey silk dress, but it looked tumbled, as if she had lain down in it, and her hair was rough and disarranged. It was the gown she had worn the previous evening, and it would almost seem as if she had done nothing to herself since going up-stairs to bed. The signs caught her father's eye, and he spoke in astonishment.

"Why—what in the world, girl? You have

never undressed yourself! Surely, you did not
pay too much respect to the wine, as some of
the men did!"

"You know better than that, sir. I was very
tired, and threw myself on the bed when I came
up: I suppose sleep overtook me. Do not allude
to it, papa, downstairs. I will soon change my
dress."

"Sleeping in your clothes does not seem to
agree with you, Mary Anne: you look as white
as if you had swallowed a doctor's shop. Do you
know anything of Cyril?—that's what I wanted
to ask you."

"No," she replied, "I have neither seen nor
heard him."

Mr. Thornycroft came to the conclusion that
Cyril had heard of the calamity, and gone out to
see about it in his curiosity. He returned to
the breakfast-room and said this. Sinnett, who
was there, turned round and spoke.

"Mr. Cyril did not sleep at home last night,
sir."

"Nonsense," responded the justice.

"He did *not*, sir," persisted Sinnett, in as
positive a tone as she dared to use.

"Not sleep at home!" cried Mr. Thornycroft,

ironically. "You must be mistaken, Sinnett. Cyril is not a night-bird," he continued, turning his fine and rather free blue eyes on the company: "he leaves late hours to his brothers."

"When Martha took up his hot water just now, and knocked, there was no reply," returned Sinnett, quietly. "So she went in, fearing he might be ill, and found the bed had not been slept in."

For Cyril, who had never willingly been guilty of loose conduct in his whole life, to sleep out from home secretly, was as remarkable a fact as the going regularly to bed at ten o'clock would have been for his brothers. Mr. Thornycroft not only felt amazement, but showed it.

"I cannot understand this at all. Richard, do you know where he can be?"

"Not in the least. I was waiting for him to come down that I might question him where he parted with Hunter."

"When did you see him last?"

"When he was going off last night with Hunter. I have not seen him since. He will turn up by-and-bye," continued Richard, carelessly. "If a fellow never has stopped out to make a night of it, that's no reason why he never may. Perhaps he came to an anchor at the Mermaid."

Clearly there was reason in this. Cyril Thornycroft might have remained out from some cause or other, though he never had before, and the gentlemen fell to their breakfast again. But for the strange and unhappy fact of Hunter's having come back to Coastdown, Mr. Thornycroft had concluded that Cyril must have walked with him to Jutpoint, and taken a bed there.

"Go up to Miss Thornycroft, Sinnett," said the justice. "She does not seem well. Perhaps she would like some tea."

Giving a look round the table first to see that nothing more was wanted (for the housekeeper liked to execute orders at her own time and will), she proceeded to Miss Thornycroft's room. The young lady then had her hair down and her dress off, apparently in the legitimate process of dressing.

"My goodness me, Miss Mary Anne, how white you look!" was the involuntary exclamation of the servant. "It is a dreadful thing, miss, but you must not take it too much to heart. It is worse for poor Mr. Hunter himself than it is for you."

Mary Anne Thornycroft, who had made a vain effort to hide her emotion and her ghastly face from the servant, opened her lips to speak, and closed them again, unable to utter a syllable.

" What a *gaby* the justice must have been to make such haste to tell her !" thought the woman. For it never occurred to Sinnett that Miss Thornycroft could have gained the information from any other source ; or, rather, it may be more correct to say that she knew it could not have been gained from any other. Sinnett, standing in the hall underneath at the moment, had heard her master's knock for admission at his daughter's door, and the colloquy that ensued—not the words, only the sound of the voices.

" The whole village is up in arms," continued Sinnett. " It is an awful murder. Hyde—"

" Don't talk of it," came the interrupting wail ; " I cannot bear it yet. Is he found ?"

" Poor wretch, yes ! with no look of a human face about him, they say," was Sinnett's answer.

" Shot down on to the Half-moon ?" shuddered Miss Thornycroft, evidently speaking more to herself than to Sinnett.

" In the fur corner of it. I'll go and bring you a cup of tea, miss. You are shaking all over."

Mary Anne put out her hand to arrest her, but she was weak, feeble, suffering, and Sinnett went on, totally regardless. In the woman's opinion there was no panacea for ills, whether mental or bodily, like a cup of strong tea, and she hastened to bring one for her young lady. The shortest way of doing this was to get it from the breakfast-room, and in went Sinnett. She was not disposed to stand on too much ceremony at the best of times, especially when put out. Occupying her position for many years as mistress of the internal economy of the Red Court Farm, she felt her sway in. it, and she was warmly condemning her master for having spoken. For Sinnett was one who liked on occasion to set those about her to rights. The large silver teapot was before the justice. Sinnett, a breakfast cup in her hand, went up and asked him to fill it.

"What a pity it is, sir, that you told Miss Thornycroft so soon; before she was well out of her bed!" began Sinnett in an under tone, as she stood waiting. "Time enough for her to have heard such a horrid thing, sir, when she had taken a bit of breakfast. There she is, shaking like a child, not able to dress herself."

"I did not tell her," returned Mr. Thorny-croft aloud.   "What are you talking of?"

"Yes, you did, sir."

"I did *not*, I tell you."

"You must have told her, sir," persisted Sinnett.   "The first thing she asked me was, whether the body was found on the Half-moon, and said it was shot down on to it.   Nobody else has been to the room but yourself."

"Take up the tea to your mistress, and don't stand cavilling here," interposed Richard, in a tone of stern command.

Justice Thornycroft brooked not contradiction from a servant.   Moreover, he began to think that his daughter must have got her information from Cyril.   He rose from table and strode up-stairs after Sinnett, following her into his daughter's room.

"Mary Anne"—in a sharp tone—"did you tell that woman I disclosed to you what had happened to Hunter?"

"No," was the reply.

"Did I tell you that anything had happened to him?"

"No, papa, you did not."

"Do you hear what Miss Thornycroft says?"

continued the magistrate, turning to the servant. "I advise you not to presume to contradict me again. If the house were in less excitement, you should come in before them all, and beg my pardon."

A ghastly look of fear had started to the features of Miss Thornycroft. "I—I heard them talking of it outside," she murmured, looking at Sinnett.

"Outside!" exclaimed Sinnett.

"Underneath, in the herb-garden," faintly added Miss Thornycroft, whose very lips were white as ashes.

"Then you did not hear of it from Cyril, Mary Anne?"

"No, papa, I have not seen Cyril at all."

Justice Thornycroft strode downstairs again. Sinnett, who did not like to be rebuked—and, in truth, rarely gave occasion for it—looked rather sullen as she put down the cup and saucer.

"Nobody has been in the side garden since I got up," cried Sinnett.

"Oh, it was before that," too hastily affirmed Miss Thornycroft. "They were strange voices," she hurriedly added, as if afraid of more questions.

Sinnett shut the door on Miss Thornycroft, and

went away ruminating.   Something like fear had
arisen to the woman's own face.

"What does it all mean ?" she asked herself,
unconsciously resting the small silver waiter on
the window-seat, as she stood looking out. " She
could not have heard anything outside in the herb-
garden, for nobody has had the key of it this
morning ; and as to people having been up here
talking of it before I was up, the poor man had
not then been found."

That some dreadful mystery existed, something
that would not bear the light of day, and in
which Miss Thornycroft was in some way mixed
up, Sinnett felt certain.   And, woman-like, she
spoke out her thoughts too freely : not in ill-
nature ; not to do harm to Miss Thornycroft or
anyone else ; but in the love of talking, in the
wish to get her own curiosity satisfied. How *had*
she learnt the news ? Sinnett wondered again
and again.   What was it that had put her into
this unnatural state of alarm and fear ?   Regret
she might feel for Robert Hunter ; horror at his
dreadful   fate—but • whence   arose   the   *fear ?*
Shrewd Sinnett finally descended, her brain in
full work.

When the party in the breakfast-room had

.concluded their meal, which they did not spare, in spite of the sight their eyes had that morning looked on, they departed in a body, each one privately hoping he should be the first to alight on Mr. Cyril. In the present stage of the affair, Cyril Thornycroft was regarded as the one only person who could throw light upon it. It did not clearly appear where he could be. Richard's suggestion of the Mermaid was an exceedingly improbable one. He was not there; he seemed not to be anywhere else; nobody appeared to have seen him since the previous night, when he was starting to walk a little way with Robert Hunter.

Mr. Thornycroft sat down in the justice room to write to the coroner, and was interrupted by his eldest son. He looked up in expectation.

" Has Cyril turned up, Richard ?"

" No, sir. Cyril's not gone far. His porte-monnaie and watch are in his room."

" Yes, I caught a sight of them myself. It is strange where he can be. I am rather uneasy."

" There's no occasion for that," returned Richard. " He must have gone on to Jutpoint. There's not a doubt of it."

" Well, I suppose it is so. The curious part is,

what brought Hunter back again when he was once fairly on the road ?   They have been suggesting at the breakfast-table that he might have forgotten something ; and I suppose it was so. But what took him to the plateau ?"

Richard had his theory on that point.   " Curiosity, unjustifiable curiosity ; possibly a wicked, dishonourable resolution to betray us, after all," were the words rising so persistently in his mind that he had some difficulty not to speak them.   He did not, however ; he wished to spare unpleasantness to his father so far as might be. The only one to whom he gave the history of what took place on the previous night before parting with Hunter, was Isaac ; and Isaac, as we know, had repeated just a word to his father. Mr. Thornycroft recurred to it now.

" What was it Isaac said about you and Hunter, Richard?   I almost forget.   That Hunter went on the plateau and saw the signal-light ?"

" Hunter saw it.   When he first quitted the house some devil's instinct took him to the plateau.   I met him as he was running down, made him promise to hold his tongue, and sent him off with Cyril.   I could have staked my

life—yes, my life," added Richard, firmly—" that
he would not have come back again."

" Was that all that passed ?"

" Oh yes, that was all," carelessly returned
Richard, who thought it well not to give the
details of the unpleasant interview.   " He and
Cyril walked away together, and I fully assumed
we had seen the colour of his ugly face for the
last time."

" And East saw them down at the Hollow, so
they must have gone that far.   Well, it's very
odd ; but I suppose Cyril will clear it up."

Mr. Thornycroft drew down his spectacles before his eyes—they had been lifted while he
talked—and went on with his note to the coroner.
Again Richard broke in, speaking abruptly.

" Sir, this affair of Hunter's must be kept dark."

" Kept dark !" echoed the justice.   " When a
man's found murdered, one can't keep it dark.
What do you mean, Dick ?"

" I mean, kept as dark as the legal proceed-
ings will allow.   Don't make more stir in it, sir,
than is absolutely necessary.   It would have been
well to keep secret his having gone on the plateau
at all ; but it's known already, and can't be
helped now.   Hush it up as much as you can."

" But why ?"

" *Hush it up,*" impressively repeated Richard,
his dark face working with some inward agitation. " *I* shall know what to say in regard to
his having gone on the plateau before departure ;
you and Isaac had better be silent. Hush it up
—hush it up ! You will be at the coroner's
right hand, and can sway him imperceptibly. It
is essential advice, father."

" What the deuce !" burst forth the magistrate, staring at his son ; " you do not fear Cyril
was the murderer of Hunter ?"

" No, thank God !" fervently answered Richard.
" Cyril would be the last in the world to
speak an unkind word, let alone shoot a man.
But, don't you see, sir—too minute enquiries
may set them on the track of something
else that was done on the Half-moon last night,
and it would not do. That confounded Kyne
has got his eyes and ears open enough, as
it is."

" By George ! there's something in that," de-
liberated the justice. " My sympathy for Hunter
put that out of my mind. All right, Dicky, now I
have the cue."

Mr. Thornycroft sealed his note to the coroner,.

despatched it, and went upstairs to Lady Ellis's room. She was up, and sitting on the sofa. He shook hands and enquired how she had rested. For a long while, in fact since the beginning of her illness, their relations with each other had been but those of common acquaintance. He was wondering whether it would be well to tell her of the catastrophe; but she had already heard of it, and sat, paler than usual, gazing at the idlers who were crowding the edge of the plateau, leaning over it in their curiosity. That unusual sight would alone have told her something was the matter.

"Is it *possible* that this can be true?" she asked, in a low tone of distress. "Is Robert Hunter really murdered?"

"It is too true, unfortunately," he answered; "at least, that he is dead. Whether murdered —as everybody has been in haste to say and assume—or whether accidentally shot, remains to be proved."

"And what are the particulars? What is known?"

But here Mr. Thornycroft would not satisfy her, or could not stay to do it. His carriage was at the door to take him to Jutpoint, where he had magisterial business that could not be postponed. Mentioning just a fact or two, he quitted the room, and found Isaac talking rather sharply to Sinnett in the hall below.

Sinnett had not allowed her doubts or her tongue to slumber. First of all she had talked to Hyde—of Miss Thornycroft's curious demeanour, of her incautious avowal, of her remarkable state of alarm and of fear; and Hyde replied by telling her to "hold her peace if she couldn't talk sense." She next, as it chanced, mentioned it to Tomlett, and he retorted that Sinnett was a fool. Sinnett felt wrathful; and in some way or other the matter penetrated to the ears of Isaac. He did not believe it; he felt sure that his sister knew nothing, and was taking Sinnett to task when Mr. Thornycroft descended.

A few hasty words from the three, and Mr. Thornycroft opened the door of his daughter's parlour, where he understood she now was. Rather to his surprise, Richard was shut in with her. It was an unusual thing for him to be indoors in the day-time. She wore a morning dress now, and looked much as usual, except that her face was pale and her hands trembled. Richard went out as they entered.

" Now, then," said the justice, " we will have
this cleared up.   Where and from whom did you
hear of this matter, Mary Anne ?"

She answered briefly, leaning her forehead on
her hand, that she had heard people talking of it
early in the morning below her window.   Sinnett,
anxious to justify herself, and very vexed that
this should have come to the ears of her masters,
said this could not be ; the key of the herb-garden was in her pocket, and nobody could have
got into it.

The plot of ground on the side of the house,
under Miss Thornycroft's window, where the herbs
were grown, was enclosed.   A small glass shed
(it was not half large enough to be called a green-
house) was at one corner of it, in which Sinnett
had some plants.   Three or four of these had
been stolen one night, and since then Sinnett had
kept the gate locked.

Miss Thornycroft, her hand held up still as if
to hide her face, persisted.   She had heard voices
underneath in the early morning, strange voices ;
it was so unusual that she quietly opened her
window to listen.   They spoke of Mr. Hunter,
and she caught distinctly the words " murder,"
and " shot down from the heights to the Half-

moon." "It was as if one man was telling another," faintly concluded Miss Thornycroft. "I
could only hope it was not true; it frightened
me terribly. As to how they could have been
in the herb-garden, I suppose they must have got
over the palisades."

"Nothing more likely, that they might talk at
leisure without interruption," cried the justice,
turning angrily on his housekeeper. "Let the
subject be dropped: do you hear, Sinnett? How
dare you attempt to raise a cabal! What's the
matter with you to-day? One would think *you*
shot him down."

Striding across the hall, the justice went out
to his restive horses, prancing and pawing the
ground in their impatience. Isaac followed him.

"If you will allow me, sir, I should like to
accompany you."

"All right, Isaac; get up."

The justice drove away, his son by his side, his
groom sitting behind, as he had once, years ago,
driven away from the gate of Mrs. Chester; but
his daughter was with him then. Isaac's errand
to Jutpoint, unavowed, was to look after Cyril.
Why it should have been so he could not have
told, then or later, but an uneasy prevision lay

on his mind that something or other was wrong, more than met the eye.

Sinnett, nettled beyond everything at her master's concluding reproach, spoken though it was in irony, and at the turn of affairs altogether, flounced off to her kitchen, leaving Miss Thorny-croft alone. She—Mary Anne Thornycroft—had made her explanation almost glibly, after the manner of one who has learnt a part by heart, and recites it. That some most awful dread was upon her—apart from the natural grief and horror arising from the murder, if it was murder—was indisputable; and Sinnett felt sure of it still.

Her face buried in her hands; her body sway-ing backwards and forwards in her chair; her whole aspect evincing dire agony now she was alone, sat Mary Anne Thornycroft. In that one past night she seemed to have aged years. The knock of a visitor aroused her; some curious gossip come to inquire and chatter and comment; and she escaped upstairs, crossing Hyde in the hall.

" I cannot see anyone, Hyde; my head aches too much."

The door of her stepmother's room was open, and Lady Ellis called to her. One single mo-

ment of rebellion, of wish to escape, and then she
remembered that she had not been in at all that
morning, and also that it was well to avoid ob-
servation just now. Lady Ellis sat as Mr. Thornycroft had left her ; her dark hair drawn simply
from her wasted face, her purple morning-gown
tied at the waist with a cord and tassel, its lace
ruffles falling over her thin white hand.

" I was just going to ring and ask you to come
up, Mary Anne. I *must* hear the particulars of
this dreadful mystery ; I cannot rest until they
are told. Look at them !"

She pointed to the heights. Dotting the plateau, peeping in at the round tower, holding
hands and waists for security as they bent forward over the edge to look at the scene of the
tragedy below, were the idlers. Mary Anne sat
down near the table, her elbow on it, her head
leaning on her hand, her eyes bent on the carpet,
and told the particulars that the world knew.
Lady Ellis heard them to the end without comment.

" But why should he have gone on the plateau
at all ?" she questioned.

" I don't know. He did go. As I stood at
the door watching him off, he turned from the

road to the plateau. I saw him. I saw him cross the railings."

" And your brother Richard saw him ?"

" Yes, as he was coming off. They stood talking for a minute or two, Richard says. Cyril came up then, and he started to walk a little way with Robert Hunter."

" But what does Cyril say ?   Where is he ?"

" He has not been home since. They suppose he went on to Jutpoint and slept there. Nothing more except this is known."

" But Mr. Hunter must have come back again ?"

" Of course he must.   It is his coming back that is so unaccountable."

" And why—why should Cyril walk to Jutpoint, unless he walked with Mr. Hunter ?" resumed Lady Ellis after a pause.

Miss Thornycroft shook her head.   It was in truth so much involved in doubt and mystery from beginning to end, that she felt unable to cope with it, even by conjecture, she said faintly. " The terrible point in it all seems to be in his having come back again."

" Nay, the terrible point is the attack upon him," dissented her step-mother.   " It might

have been an accidental shot, after all. At
what hour was it supposed to take place?"

Miss Thornycroft could not say. "Of course
—yes—it might have been only accidental," she
assented with whitening lips.

"Mary Ann, how ill you look!"

"Do I? It frightened me, you see. And I
have a dreadful headache," she added, rising to
escape those eyes bent on her with so much
curiosity. "I must go and lie down on the bed,
if you will spare me."

"Lie on my sofa," said Lady Ellis.

"No, thank you. Shut in by myself, I may
get to sleep."

"Tell me one thing," and Lady Ellis laid her
hand on her step-daughter's arm. "Is any one
suspected?"

"No; oh no."

"I suppose, Mary Ann, it is quite sure that
he is *dead?*"

A faint cry at the mockery of the almost sug-
gested hope escaped Mary Anne's lips. When
the surgeon saw him at eight o'clock that morning, he thought he must have been dead about
ten hours.

Lady Ellis leaned back in her chair when she

was left alone, her eyes closed, her wan hands clasped meekly on her bosom.

"Ah! was he fit to go? was he fit to go?" she murmured, the thought having lain on her as a great dream of agony. "Had it been Cyril Thornycroft, there could be no doubt. But *he* —— ? Perhaps he was changed, as I am," she resumed after a long pause. "Oh! yes, yes, it might have been so; Robert Hunter might have been READY. Thank God that he gave me his forgiveness last night!"

CHAPTER IV.

THE coroner's inquest was held on the Wednesday. Nothing could exceed the state of ferment that Coastdown was in: not altogether from the fact of the murder itself—for murder it was universally assumed to be, and *was*—but also from one or two strange adjuncts that surrounded it. The first of these was the prolonged and unaccountable absence of Cyril Thornycroft; the second arose from sundry rumours rife in the town. It was whispered on the Tuesday that two or three witnesses had been present when the deed was committed; that they had seen it done; and the names of these, scarcely breathed at first, but gathering strength as the day wore on, were at length spoken freely : Miss Thornycroft, Miss Chester, and Captain Copp's maidservant, Sarah Ford.

Whether the reports arose, in the first place,

in consequence of Sinnett's talking; whether Sarah Ford had spoken a hasty word on the Monday morning, in her surprise and shock at what she heard; or whether the facts had gone about through those strange instincts of suspicion that do sometimes arise in the most extraordinary manner, nobody can tell how or whence, was not yet known. But the rumours reached the ear of the summoning officer, and at ten o'clock on the Tuesday night that functionary delivered his mandates—one at the Red Court Farm, two at Captain Copp's, for these witnesses to attend the inquest. Speaking afterwards at the Mermaid of what he had done, the excitement knew no bounds.

Speculation was rife in regard to the most strange absence of Cyril Thornycroft. But not quite at first—not, in fact, until the Wednesday morning—was any unpleasant feeling connected with it. It might have been in men's minds—who could say it had not?—but on the Wednesday it began to be spoken. Was Cyril the guilty man? Had *he*, in a scuffle or else, fired the shot that killed Hunter?

The taint was carried in a whisper to the Red Court Farm. It staggered Mr. Thornycroft; it drove Isaac speechless; but Richard, in his

usual fashion, went into a white heat of indignation. Cyril, who was one of the best men on
the face of the earth!—who lived, as everybody
knew, a gentle and blameless life, striving to
follow, so far as might be, the example his
Master set when He came on earth!—who would
not hurt a fly, who was ever seeking to soothe
others battling with the world's troubles, and help
them on the road to Heaven!—*he* kill Robert
Hunter! Richard's emotion overwhelmed him,
and his lips turned white as he spoke it.

All very true: if ever a man strove to walk
near to God, it was certainly Cyril Thornycroft;
and Richard's hearers acknowledged it. But—
and this they did not say—good men had been
overtaken by temptation, by crime, before now;
and, after all, this might have been a pure accident. If Cyril Thornycroft were innocent, argued
Coastdown, why did he run away? Of course,
his prolonged absence, if voluntary, was the great
proof against him: even unprejudiced people
admitted that. Mr. Thornycroft and his sons
had another theory, and were not uneasy. It
was not convenient to speak of it to the world;
but they fully believed Cyril would return home
in a week or two, safe and sound; and they also,

one and all, implicitly believed that he was not
only guiltless of the death of Robert Hunter, but
ignorant of its having taken place.   The fact of
his having no money with him went for nothing
—it has been mentioned that his purse was left
in his room,—if Cyril had gone where they suspected, he could have what money he pleased for
the asking.

In this state of excitement and uncertainty,
Wednesday morning dawned.   As the hour for
the coroner's inquest drew near, all the world
assembled round the Mermaid : to see the
coroner and jury go in would be something.
Captain Copp stumped about in a condition of
wrath that promised momentary explosion, arising from the fact that his " women-kind " should
be subpœnaed to give evidence on a land murder.
What they might have to say about it, or what
they had not to say, the captain was unable to
get at; his questioning had been in vain:
Sarah was silent and sullen; Anna Chester
white and shivering, as if some great blow had
fallen on her; and this unsatisfactory state of
things did not tend to increase the captain's
equanimity.   He had been originally summoned
to serve on the inquest, but when the officer came

to the house at ten on the Tuesday night, he told
him he had perhaps better not serve. All this
was as bitter aloes to the merchant captain.

The inquest took place in the club-room of the
Mermaid, the coroner taking his seat at the head
of its long table covered with green baize, while
the jury ranged themselves round it. Justice
Thornycroft was seated at the right hand of the
coroner. They had viewed the body, which lay
in an adjoining room, just as it had been brought
up.

The first witness called was Mr. Supervisor
Kyne, he having been the first to discover the
calamity. With break of day on the Monday
morning he went on the plateau. Happening
to look over as far as he could stretch, he saw
what he thought to be Mr. Hunter asleep: the
face was hidden from him as he stood above, but
he knew him by his coat. Going round to the
Half-moon beach, having been joined on his way
by one or two fishermen, they discovered that the
poor gentleman was not asleep, but dead : in fact
that he had been killed, and in a most frightful
manner.

The surgeon who had been called to examine the
body spoke next. The cause of death was a shot,

he said. The bullet had entered the face, gone through the brain, and passed out at the crown of the head. Death must have been instantaneous, he thought: and the face had also been very much defaced by the jagged points of the rock in falling. In answer to the coroner, the surgeon said he should think it had been many hours dead when he was called to see it at half-past seven in the morning: nine or ten at least.

The next witness was Mr. Thornycroft, who stood up to give his evidence. He spoke to the fact of the young man's having been his guest for a short while at the Red Court: that he had intended to leave on the Sunday night by the half-past eight omnibus for Jutpoint, to catch the train; but had missed it. He then said he would walk it, wished them good-bye, and left with that intention. He knew no more.

Mr. Thornycroft sat down again, and Richard was called. He confirmed his father's evidence, and gave some in addition. On the Sunday night he quitted the dining-room soon after the deceased, and went outside for a stroll. There he saw Hunter, who appeared to have been on the plateau. They stood together a few moments talking, and just as they were parting Cyril came up. He, Cyril, said he would walk a little way with Hunter, and they turned away together.

"To walk to Jutpoint?" interposed the coroner.

"Yes: speaking of Hunter. Of course I supposed my brother would turn back almost immediately."

"Were they upon angry terms one with the other?"

"Certainly not."

"And you never saw either of them afterwards?"

"No," replied Richard, in a low tone—which the room set down to uneasiness on the score of Cyril's absence. "I went indoors then."

"You are sure that the deceased was then starting, positively starting, on his walk to Jutpoint?"

"I am quite certain. There is no doubt of it whatever."

"What, then, caused him to come back again?"

"I am quite unable to conjecture. It is to me one of the strangest points connected with this strange business."

Cause, indeed, had Richard Thornycroft to say so! He, of all others, he alone, knew of the oath taken by Hunter *not* to come back; of the danger Hunter knew he would run in attempting it. To the very end of Richard's life—as it seemed to him now—would the thing be a mystery to his mind: unless Cyril should be able to throw light upon it.

Richard Thornycroft had no further testimony to offer, and Isaac was next examined. He could say no more than his father had said; not having seen Hunter at all since the latter quitted the dining-room. Of the subsequent events of the night, he said he knew personally nothing: he was not out of doors. The fisherman, East, next appeared, and testified to having seen Cyril Thornycroft and Mr. Hunter together, as before stated.

"Were you looking out for them?" asked a sapient juryman.

"Looking out for 'em?" repeated East. "Lawk love ye, I warn't a-looking out for nobody. I'd not have noticed 'em, maybe, but for Mr. Hunter's white coat that he'd got buttoned on him. One couldn't be off seeing *that*."

"Call Cyril Thornycroft," said the coroner.

The calling of Cyril Thornycroft was a mere form, as the coroner was aware. He had learnt all the unpleasant rumours and suspicions attaching to Cyril's absence; had no doubt formed his own opinion on the point. But he was careful not to avow that opinion; perhaps also not to press for any evidence that might tend to confirm it, out of regard to his old friend, Justice Thornycroft.

"Have you any suggestion to offer as to your son's absence?" he asked in a considerate tone of the magistrate.

Mr. Thornycroft stood up to answer. His countenance was clear and open, his fine upright form raised to its full height : evidently *he* attached no suspicion to his son's non-return.

"I think it will be found that he has only gone to see some friends who live at a distance, and that a few days will bring him home again. My reasons for this belief are good, though I would rather not state them publicly ; they are conclusive to my own mind, and to the minds of my two elder sons. And I beg to say that I affirm this in all honour, as a magistrate and a gentleman."

Again the coroner paused. " Do you con-

sider, Mr. Thornycroft, that your son preme-
ditated this visit?"

"No; or he would have spoken of it. I
think that circumstances must have caused him
to depart on it suddenly."

Mr. Thornycroft was thinking of one class of
"circumstances," the coroner and jury of another.
They could only connect any circumstances,
causing sudden departure, with the tragedy of
the night, with a sense of guilt. Mr. Thornycroft knew of another outlet.

"Is it usual for him to leave his watch
and purse on the drawers, sir?" asked a
juror.

"It is not unusual. He does so sometimes
when changing his coat and waistcoat for dinner:
not intentionally, but from forgetfulness. He is
absent-minded at the best of times: not at all
practical as his brothers are."

"But what would he do without money on a
journey?" persisted the gentleman.

Mr. Thornycroft paused for a moment, considering his answer. It was exceedingly unfortunate that he could not speak out freely: Cyril's
reputation had suffered less.

"The fact of his having left his purse at home

does not prove he has no money with him," said the justice. "In fact, I believe he keeps his porte-monnaie in his pocket from habit more than anything else, and carries his money loose. Most men, so far as I know, like to do so. I examined the porte-monnaie this morning, and found it empty."

There was a slight laugh at this, hushed immediately. Mr. Thornycroft, finding nothing further was asked him, sat down again.

"Call Sarah Ford," said the coroner.

Sarah Ford came in, and Captain Copp, who made one of the few spectators, struck his wooden leg irascibly on the floor of the room : a respectable, intelligent-looking woman, quietly attired in a straw bonnet, a brown shawl with flowered border, with a white handkerchief in her gloved hands. She did not appear to be in the least put out at having to appear before the coroner and jury, and gave her evidence with the most perfect independence.

The coroner looked at his notes; not of the evidence already given, which his clerk was taking down, but of some he had brought to refresh his memory.

"Do you recollect last Sunday evening, witness ?" he asked, when a few preliminary questions had been gone through.

" What should hinder me ?" returned the witness, ever ready with her tongue. " It's not so long ago."

" Where did you go to that evening ?"

" I went nowhere but to Justice Thornycroft's."

" For what purpose did you go there ?"

" To fetch Miss Chester. She was to have been sent for at eight o'clock, but master and mistress forgot it. When it was on the stroke of nine they told me to go for her."

" Which you did ?"

" Which I did, and without stopping to put anything on."

" Did you meet anybody as you went ?"

" Yes ; nearly close to the Red Court gates I met Mr. Hunter and young Cyril Thornycroft."

" Walking together towards the village ?" interposed the coroner.

" Walking on that way. Mr. Hunter was buttoning himself up tight in that blessed fine coat of his."

" Did they seem angry with each other ?"

" No, sir ; they were talking pleasantly. Mr.

Cyril was saying to the other that if he stepped out he would be at Jutpoint by half-past ten. That was before they came close, but the air was clear and brought out the sound of their voices."

" Did they speak to you ?"

" I spoke to them. I asked Mr. Hunter if he had lost the omnibus, for, you must understand, Miss Chester had said in the afternoon that he was going by it, and he said ' Yes, he had, and had got to walk it.' So I wished him a good journey."

" Was that all ?"

" All that he said. Mr. Cyril asked me was I going to the Court, and I said ' Yes, I was, to fetch Miss Chester,' and that ' master was in a tantrum at its being so late.' (An irascible word from Captain Copp.) With that they went their way and I went mine."

" After that, you reached the Red Court ?"

" Of course I reached it."

" Well, what happened there ?   Relate it in full."

" Nothing particular happened that I know of, except that the servants gave me some mulled wine."

" While you were waiting ?"

" Yes, while I was waiting ; and a fine time Miss
Chester kept me, although I told her about the
anger at home.   She—"

" Stay a moment, witness.   How long do you
think it was ?"

" A quarter of an hour or twenty minutes.
Quite that."

" And now go on.   We know the details, witness," added the coroner, significantly.   " I tell
you this, that you may relate them without being
questioned at every sentence ; it will save time."

Sarah looked at him.   That he was speaking
the truth was self-evident ; and she prepared to
tell her story consecutively, without any sup-
pression.   The coroner was impatient.

" Speak up, witness.   Miss Thornycroft went
out with you.   What induced her to go ?"

" I suppose it was a freak she took," replied
the witness.   " When they said Miss Chester was
ready I went into the hall, and Miss Thornycroft,
in a sort of joke (I didn't think she meant it)
said she would come out with her.   Miss Chester
asked her how she would get back again, and she
answered, laughing, that she'd run back, to be
sure, nobody was about to see her.   Well, she
put on her garden-bonnet, which hung there,

and a shawl, and we came away, all three or us.
In going out at the gates they both turned on
the waste land, towards the plateau. I saw 'em
stop and stare up on it, as if they saw something;
and I wished they'd just stare at our way home
instead, for I was not over warm, lagging there.
Presently one of them said to me—for I had followed—'Sarah, do look, is not that Robert
Hunter walking about there?' 'My eyes is too
chilled to see so far, young ladies,' says I; 'what
should bring Robert Hunter there, when I met
him as I came along, speeding on his journey to
Jutpoint?' 'I can see that it *is* Robert Hunter,'
returned Miss Thornycroft; 'I can see him quite
distinct on that high ground against the sky.'
And with that they told me to wait there, and
they'd just run up and frighten him. Precious
cross I was, and I took off my black stuff apron
and threw it over my head, shawl fashion, thinking what a fool I was to come out on a cold
frosty night without——"

"Confine yourself to the evidence," sternly
interrupted the coroner.

"Well," proceeded Sarah, who remained as
cool and equable before the coroner and jury as
she would have been in her own kitchen, "I

7—2

doubled my apron over my head, and down I sat on that red stone which rises out of the ground there like a low milestone. In a minute or two somebody comes running on to the plateau, as if following the young ladies——"

"From what direction, witness?"

"I think from that of the Red Court Farm. It might have been from that of the village, but I think it was the other; I am not sure either way. You see, I had got my apron right over me, and my head bent down on my knees, afeard of catching the face-ache, and I never heard anything till he was on the plateau. When I saw him he was near the Round Tower, going straight up to it, as it were; so he might have come from either way."

"Did you recognise him?"

"No; I didn't try to. I saw it was a man, through the slit I had left in my apron. He was going fast, but stealthily, hardly letting his shoes touch the ground, as if he was up to no good. And I was not sorry to see him go there, for thinks I, he'll hurry back my young ladies."

"Witness—pay attention—were there no signs by which you could recognise that man?

How was he dressed? As a gentleman?—as a sailor?—as a——"

"As a gentleman, for all I saw to the contrary," replied the witness, unceremoniously interrupting the coroner's question. "If I had known he was going on to the plateau to murder Mr. Hunter, you may be sure I'd have looked at him sharp enough."

"For all you saw to the contrary," repeated the coroner, taking up the words; "what do you mean by that?"

"Well, what I mean is, I suppose, that he might have been a gentleman or he might not. The fact is, I never noticed his dress at all. I think the clothes were dark, and I think he had leggings on—which are worn by common people and gentlemen alike down here. The stars was rather under a cloud at the time, and so was my temper."

"Honestly acknowledged," said the coroner. "What sized man was he?—tall or short?"

"Very tall."

"Taller than—Mr. Cyril Thornycroft, for instance?"

"A great deal taller."

"You are sure of this?"

"I am sure and certain. Why else should I say so?"

"Go on with your evidence."

"A minute or so afterwards, as I sat with my back to the plateau and my head in my lap, I heard a gun go off behind me."

"Did that startle you?" asked an interrupting juryman.

"No, I am not nervous. If I had known it was let off on the plateau it might have startled me, on account of the young ladies being there; but I thought it was only from some passing vessel."

"It is singular you should have thought so lightly of it. It is not common to hear a gun fired on a Sunday night."

"You'd find it common enough if you lived here, sir. What with rabbit and other game shooters, and signals from boats, it is nothing in this neighbourhood to hear a gun go off, and it's what nobody pays any attention to."

"Therefore you did not?"

"Therefore I did not. And the apron I had got muffled over my ears made the sound appear further off than it really was. But close upon the noise came an awful cry; and that was followed by a shrill scream, as if from a woman. That startled me, if you like, and I jumped up, and threw off my apron, and looked on to the plateau. I could not see anything; neither the man nor the young ladies; so I thought it time to go and search after them. I had got nearly up to the Round Tower, that ruined wall, breast high, which is on the plateau——"

" You need not explain," said the coroner, " we know the place."

" When a man darted out from the shade of it," continued the witness. " He cut across to the side of the plateau next the village, and disappeared down that dangerous steep path in the cliffs, which nobody afore, I guess, ever ventured down but in broad daylight."

" Was it the same man you saw just before running on to the plateau ?"

" Of course it was."

" By what marks did you know him again ?"

" By no marks at all. I should not know the man from Adam. My own senses told me it was the same, because there was no other man on the plateau."

" Your own senses will not do to speak from. Remember, witness, you are on your oath."

" Whether I am on my oath or off it, I should speak the truth," was the response of the imperturbable witness.

" What next ?"

" I stood looking at the man ; that is, at where he had disappeared ; expecting he was pitching down head foremost and getting half killed, at the pace he was going, when Miss Thornycroft laid hold of me, shaking and crying, almost beside herself with terror. Then I found that Miss Chester had fainted away, and was lying like one dead on the frosty grass inside the Round Tower."

" What account did they give of this ?"

" They gave none to me. Miss Chester, when she came to herself, was too much shook to do it, and Miss Thornycroft was no better. I thought they had been startled by the man ; I never thought worse ; and I did not hear of the murder till the next morning. They told me not to say anything about it at home, or it would be known they had been on the plateau. So Miss Thornycroft ran back to the Red Court, and I went home with Miss Chester."

" What else do you know about the matter ?"

" I don't know any more myself. I have heard plenty."

The witness's "hearing" was dispensed with, and Captain Copp was requested to stand up and answer a question. The captain's face, as he listened to the foregoing evidence, was something ludicrous to look upon.

"What account did Miss Chester and your servant give you of this transaction?" demanded the coroner.

"What account did they give me?" spluttered Captain Copp, to whom the question sounded as the most intense aggravation. "They gave me none. This is the first time my ears have heard it. I only wish I had been behind them with a cat-o'-nine-tails"—shaking his stick in a menacing manner—"I'd have taught them to go gampusing on to the plateau at night, after sweethearts! I'll send my niece back to whence she came; her father was a clergyman, Mr. Coroner, a rector of a parish. And that vile bumboat-woman, Sarah, with her apron over her head, shall file out of my quarters this day; a she-pirate, a———"

The coroner interposed. But what with Captain Copp's irascibility and his real ignorance of the whole transaction, nothing satisfactory could be obtained from him, and the next witness called was Miss Chester. A lady-like, interesting girl, thought those of the spectators who had not previously seen her. She gave her evidence in a sad, low tone, trembling the whole of the time with inward terror. To a sensitive mind, as hers was, the very fact of having to give her name as Anna Chester when it was Anna Thornycroft, would have been enough alarm. But there was worse than that.

Her account of their going on to the plateau was the same as Sarah's. It was "done in the impulse of the moment," to "frighten," or "speak to," Robert Hunter, who was at its edge. (A groan from Captain Copp.) That they halted for a moment at the Round Tower, and then found that a man was following them on to the plateau, so they ran inside to hide themselves.

" Who was that man ?" asked the coroner.

" I don't know," was the faint reply. " I am near-sighted."

" Did you look at him ?"

" We peeped out, round the wall. At least, Miss Thornycroft did. I only looked for a moment."

" Proceed, witness, if you please."

" He had come quite close when I looked, and
—then——"

" Then what ?" said the coroner, looking
searchingly at the witness, who seemed unable
to continue. " You must speak up, young
lady."

" Then I saw him with a pistol—and he fired
it off—and I was so terrified that I fainted, and
remembered no more. It all passed in a
moment."

" A good thing if he had shot off your two
figure-heads !" burst forth Captain Copp, who
was immediately silenced.

" Was he tall or short, this man ?"

" Tall."

" Did you know him ?" proceeded the coroner.

" Oh no, no," was Anna's answer, putting up
her hands, as if to ward off the approach of some
terror, and she burst into a fit of hysterical
crying.

She was conducted from the room. Isaac
Thornycroft advanced to give her his arm, but
she turned from him and took that of the
doctor, who was standing by. An impression was
left on the mind of one or two of the listeners
that Miss Chester could have told more.

With the subsiding of the hubbub, the coroner resumed his business.

"Call Mary Anne Thornycroft."

Miss Thornycroft appeared, led in by her brother Richard. She wore a rich black silk dress, a velvet mantle, and small bonnet with blue flowers. Her face was of a deadly white, her lips were compressed; but she delivered her evidence with composure (unlike Miss Chester), in a low, deliberate, thoughtful tone. Her account of their going on to the plateau, and running inside the Round Tower at the approach of some man, who appeared to be following them, was the same as that given by the last witness. The coroner inquired if she had recognised Robert Hunter.

"Yes," was the reply. "I saw the outline of his face and figure distinctly, and knew him. I recognised him first by the coat he had on; it was quite conspicuous in the starlight. He was standing on the brink, apparently looking out over the sea.

"That was before you saw the man who came running on to the plateau?"

"Yes."

"Who was that man?"

Mary Anne Thornycroft laid her hand upon her heart, as if pressing down its emotion, before she answered.

" I cannot tell."

" Did you not know him ?"

" No."

" Upon your oath ?"

Miss Thornycroft again pressed her hands, both hands, upon her bosom, and a convulsive twitching was perceptible in her throat ; but she replied, in a low tone, " Upon my oath."

" Then, he was a stranger ?"

She bowed her rigid face in reply, for the white strained lips refused to answer. Motions are no answers for coroners, and this one spoke again.

" I ask you whether he was a stranger ?"

" Yes."

" From what direction did he come ?"

" I do not know. He was near the Round Tower before I saw him."

" You saw him draw the pistol and fire ?"

" Yes."

" Now, young lady, I am going to ask you a painful question, but the ends of justice demand that you should answer it. Was that man your brother, Cyril Thornycroft ?"

"No," she answered, in the sharp tone of earnest truth, "I swear it was not—I swear it before Heaven. The man bore no resemblance whatever to my brother Cyril; he was at least a head taller."

" Did he aim at Robert Hunter?"

" I cannot say. Robert Hunter was standing with his face towards us then, and I saw him fall back, over the precipice."

" With a yell, did he not?"

" Yes, with a yell."

" What then?"

" I cannot tell what. I believe I shrieked— I cannot remember. I next saw the man running away across the plateau."

" The witness Sarah Ford's evidence would seem to say that he lingered a few moments after firing the pistol—before escaping," interposed the coroner.

" It is possible. I was too terrified to retain a clear recollection of what passed. I remember seeing him run away, and then Sarah Ford came up."

" Should you recognise that man again?"

Miss Thornycroft hesitated. The room waited in breathless silence for her answer. " I believe not," she said; "it was only starlight. I am sure not."

At this moment, an inqusitive juryman spoke up. He wished to know how it was that Miss Thornycroft and the other young lady had never mentioned these facts until to-day, when they had been drawn from them, as it were, by their oath.

"Because," Miss Thornycroft replied, with, if possible, a deeper shade of paleness arising to her face—"because they did not care that their foolish freak of going on to the plateau should come to the knowledge of their friends."

"Glad they have some sense of shame left in them," cried Captain Copp.

The inquisitive juryman was not quite satisfied. He asked to have the maid-servant recalled; and, when she appeared, put the same question to her. Why had *she* not told of it?"

Why didn't she tell! was the independent retort. Did the gentlemen think she was going to bleat out to the world what the young ladies had seen, when they did not choose to tell of it themselves, and so bring 'em here to be browbeat and questioned, as they had all been this day? Not she. She was only sorry other folks had ferreted it out, and told.

Very little evidence was forthcoming, none of consequence to the general reader. Supervisor Kyne volunteered a statement about smuggling, which nobody understood, and Justice Thorny-croft at once threw ridicule upon. The coroner cut it short, and proceeded to charge the jury. Primarily remarking that, if the evidence was to be believed, Cyril Thornycroft must be held exempt from the suspicion whispered against him, he went on: If they thought a wicked, deliberate act of murder had been committed, they were to bring in a verdict to that effect; and if they thought it had not, they were not to bring it in so. Grateful for this luminous advice, the jury proceeded to deliberate—that is, they put their heads together, and spoke for some minutes in an undertone; and then intimated that they had agreed upon their verdict.

"Wilful murder against some person or per-sons unknown."

CHAPTER V.

FILING out of the room in groups, came the crowd who had filled it. The day had changed. The brightness of the morning was replaced by a wintry afternoon of grey sky; the air blew keen; snow began to fall. The eager spectators put up their umbrellas, if they happened to possess any, and stood to talk in excited whispers.

Crossing to the waste land, the roundabout road she chose to take on her way home, was Anna Chester. Sarah had gone striding up the nearest way; Captain Copp had been laid hold of by Supervisor Kyne, whose grievance on the score of the smugglers was sore; and Anna was alone. Her veil drawn over her white face, her eyes wearing a depth of trouble never yet seen in their sweetness, went she, looking neither to the right nor left, until she was overtaken by Miss Thornycroft.

" Anna !"

" Mary Anne !"

For a full minute they stood, looking into each other's faces of fear and pain. And then the latter spoke, a rising sob of emotion catching her breath.

" Thank you for what you have done this day, Anna! I was in doubt before; I did not know how much you had seen that night; whether you had not mercifully been spared all by the fainting fit. But now that you have given your evidence, I see how much I have to thank you for. Thank you truly. We have both forsworn ourselves: you less than I; but surely Heaven will forgive us in such a cause."

" Let us never speak of it again," murmured Anna. " I don't think I can bear it."

" Just a word first—to set my mind at rest," returned Miss Thornycroft, as she stood grasping Anna's hand in hers. " How much did you see ? Did you see the pistol fired ?"

" I saw only that. It was at the moment I looked out round the wall. The flash drove me back again. That and the cry that broke from Robert Hunter: upon which I fainted for the first time in my life."

" And you—recognised him—him who fired the pistol?" whispered Miss Thornycroft, glancing cautiously round as the words issued from her bloodless lips.

" Yes, I fear so."

It was quite enough. Qualified though the avowal was, Mary Anne saw that she could have spoken decisively. The two unhappy girls, burdened with their miserable secret, looked into each other's faces that sickness and terror had rendered white. Anna, as if in desperation to have her fears confirmed where no confirmation was needed, broke the silence.

" It—was—your—brother."

" Yes."

" Isaac."

Miss Thornycroft opened her lips to speak, and closed them again. She turned her head away.

" You will not betray him—and us, Anna? You will ever be cautious—silent?"

" I will be cautious and silent always; I will guard the secret jealously."

A sharp pressure of the hand in ratification of the bargain, and they parted, Anna going on her solitary way.

" Will I guard the secret! Heaven alone

knows how much heavier lies the obligation on
me to do so than on others," wailed Anna.
" May God help me to bear it !"

Quick steps behind her, and she turned, for
they had a ring that she knew too well. Pressing onwards through the flakes of snow came
Isaac Thornycroft. Anna set off to run ; it was
in the lonely spot by the churchyard.

"Anna ! Anna ! Don't you know me ?"

Not a word of answer. She only ran the
faster—as if she could hope to outstep him !
Isaac, with his long, fleet strides, overtook her
with ease, and laid his hand upon her shoulder.

Like a stag brought to bay, she turned upon
him, with her terror-stricken face, more ghastly,
more trembling than it had yet been ; and by a
dexterous movement freed herself.

" Why, Anna, what is the matter ? Why do
you run from me ?"

" There's my uncle," she panted. " Don't
speak to me—don't come after me."

And sure enough, as Isaac turned, he dis-
tinguished Captain Copp at a distance. Anna
had set off to run again like a wild hare, and was
half-way across the heath. Isaac turned slowly
back, passed the captain with a nod, and went

on, wondering. What had come to Anna? Why did she fly from him?

He might have wondered still more had he been near her in her flight. Groans of pain were breaking from her; soft low moans of anguish; sighs, and horribly perplexing thoughts; driving her to a state of utter despair.

For, according to the testimony of her own eyes that ill-fated night, Anna, you see, believed the murderer to be her husband. Miss Thornycroft had now confirmed it. And, not to keep you in more suspense than can be helped, we must return to that night for a few brief moments.

When Richard Thornycroft darted into the subterranean passage with the intention of warning his brother Isaac, before he reached its end the question naturally occurred to him, *Why* stop the boats, now Hunter is off? and he turned back again. So much has been already said. But half-way down the passage he again vacillated— a most uncommon thing in Richard Thornycroft, but the episode with Hunter had wellnigh scared his senses away. Turning about again, he retraced his steps and called to Isaac.

A private conference ensued. Richard told

all without reserve, down to the point where he
had watched Hunter away, under the surveillance
of Cyril.   " Will it be better to stop the boats or
not ?" he asked.

" There is not the slightest cause for stopping
them, that I see," returned Isaac, who had listened
attentively.   " Certainly not.   Hunter is gone ;
and if he were not, I do not think, by what you
say, that he would attempt to interfere further ;
he'd rather turn his back a mile the other way."

" Let them come on then," decided Richard.

" They are already, I expect, putting off from
the ship."

Isaac Thornycroft remained at his work ;
Richard went back again up the passage.   Not
quickly ; some latent doubt, whence arising he
could not see or trace, lingered on his mind still
—his better angel perhaps urging him from the
road he was going.   Certain it was : he remembered it afterwards even more vividly than he
felt it then : that a strong inclination lay upon
him to stop the work for that night.   But it
appeared not to hold reason, and was disregarded.

He emerged from the subterranean passage,
lightly shut the trap-door—which could be

opened from the inside at will, when not
fastened down—and took his way to the plateau
to watch against intruders. This would bring
it to about the time that the two young ladies
had gone there, and Sarah, her apron over her
head, had taken her place on the low red stone.
In her evidence the woman had said it might be
a quarter of an hour or twenty minutes since
she met Robert Hunter starting on his journey;
it had taken Richard about that time to do since
what he had done; and it might have taken
Robert Hunter about the same space (or rather
less) to walk quickly to the wherry, *and come back
again.* And come back again! Richard Thornycroft could have staked his life, had the question
occurred to him, that Hunter would not come
back : he never supposed any living man, calling
himself a gentleman, could be guilty of so great
treachery. But the doubt never presented itself
to him for a moment.

What then was his astonishment, as he ran
swiftly and stealthily (escaping the sight of Sarah
Ford, owing, no doubt, to her crouching posture
on the stone, and the black apron on her head)
up the plateau, to see Robert Hunter? He
was at its edge, at the corner farthest from the

village; was looking out steadily over the sea, as if watching for the boats and their prey. Richard verily thought he must be in a dream : he stood still and strained his eyes, wondering if they deceived him; and then as ugly a word broke from him as ever escaped the lips of man.

Thunderstruck with indignation, with dismay, half mad at the fellow's despicable conduct, believing that if any in the world ever merited shooting, he did; nay, believing that the fool must court death to be there after his, Richard's, warning promise; overpowered with fury, with passion, Richard Thornycroft stood in the shade of the Round Tower, his eyes glaring, his white teeth showing themselves from between the drawn lips.   At that same moment Robert Hunter, after stooping to look over the precipice, turned round; the ugly fur on the breast of his coat very conspicuous. May Richard Thornycroft be forgiven !   With a second hissing oath, he drew the pistol from his breast-pocket, pointed it with his unerring hand, and fired; and the ill-fated man fell over the cliff with a yelling cry. Another shriek, more shrill, arose at Richard's elbow from the shade of the Round Tower.

"S   c u.:sed sea-bird," he muttered.   " *He*

has got his deserts. I would be served so myself, if I could thus have turned traitor!"

But what was it seized Richard's arm? Not a sea-bird. It was his sister Mary Anne. "*You* here!" he cried, with increased passion. "What the fury!—have you all turned mad to-night?"

"You have murdered him!" she cried, in a dread whisper—for how could she know that Anna Chester had fallen senseless and could not hear her?—"you have murdered Robert Hunter!"

"I have," he answered. "He is dead, and more than dead. If the shot did not take effect, the fall would kill him."

"Oh, Richard, say it was an accident!" she moaned, very nearly bereft of reason in her shock of horror. "What madness came over you?"

"He earned it of his own accord; earned it deliberately. I held my pistol to his head before, this night, and I spared him. I had him on his knees to me, and he took an oath to be away from this place instantly, and to be silent. I told him if he broke it, if he lingered here but for a moment, I would put the bullet into him. I saw him off; I sent Cyril with him to speed him on his road; and—see!—the fool came back again. I was right to do it."

"I will denounce you!" she fiercely uttered, anger getting the better of other feelings. "Ay, though you are my brother, Richard Thornycroft! I will raise the hue and cry upon you."

"You had better think twice of that," he answered, shaking her arm in his passion. "If you do, you must raise it against your father and your father's house!"

"What do you mean?" she asked, quailing, for there was a savage earnestness in his words which told of startling truth.

"Girl! see you no mystery? can't you fathom it? You would have aided Hunter in discovering the smugglers: see you not that *we* are the smugglers? We are running a cargo now—now" —and his voice rose to a hoarse shriek as he pointed to the Half-moon, "and he would have turned Judas to us! He was on the watch there, on the plateau's edge, doing traitor's work for Kyne."

"He did not know it was you he would have denounced," she faintly urged, gathering in the sense of his revelation to her sinking heart.

"He did know it. The knowledge came to

him to-night.   He was abject enough before me,
the coward, and swore he would be silent, and be
gone from hence there and then.   But his traitor's
nature prevailed, and he has got his deserts.
Now go and raise the hue and cry upon us !
Bring your father to a felon's bar."

Mary Anne Thornycroft, with a despairing cry,
sank down on the grass at her brother's feet.
He was about to raise her, rudely enough it must
be confessed, rather than tenderly, when his eye
caught the form of some one advancing ; he
darted off at right angles across the plateau, and
descended recklessly the dangerous path.

The intruder was Sarah.   Miss Thornycroft,
passing off her own emotion as the effect of fear
at the shot, though scarcely knowing how she
contrived not to betray herself, remembered
Anna.   She lay within the walls in a fainting-
fit.   Only as they went in was consciousness
beginning to return to her.   It must be mentioned that at this stage Sarah did not know any
one had been killed.

"Who was the man ?" asked Sarah of Miss
Thornycroft.

"Did you see him ?" was the only answer.

"Not to know him, miss ; only at a distance.

A regular fool he must be to fire off guns at night, to frighten folks! Was it a stranger?"

"Yes." Mary Anne wiped the dew from her cold brow as she told the lie.

They took their departure, Sarah promising not to say they had been on the plateau—to hold her tongue, in short, as to the events of the night, shot and all. But a chance passer-by who had heard the report, saw them descend. It might have been through him the news got wind.

Mary Anne Thornycroft went in. Sounds of ughter and glee proceeded from the dining-room as she passed it, and she dragged her shaking limbs upstairs to her chamber, and shut herself in with her dreadful secret. Anna Chester with *her* secret turned to the heath, even one more dreadful; for in the momentary glimpse she caught of the man who drew the pistol, as he stood partly with his back to her, she had recognised, as she fully believed, her husband Isaac. Had the impression wanted confirmation in her mind—which it did not—the tacit admission of his sister, now alluded to, supplied it. Miss Thornycroft had opened her lips to correct her, " not Isaac, but Richard ;" and closed them again without saying it. Thought is quick; and a dim idea flew through her brain, that to divert suspicion from Richard might add to his safety. It was not *her* place to denounce him; nay, her duty lay in screening him. Terribly though she detested and deplored the crime, she was still his sister.

And the poor dead body had lain unseen where it fell, in the remote corner of the plateau. The smugglers ran their cargo, passing within a few yards of the dark angle where it lay, and never saw it.

The funeral took place on the Friday, and Robert Hunter was buried within sight of the place from whence he had been shot down. Any one standing on that ill-fated spot could see the grave in the churchyard corner, close by the tomb of the late Mrs. Thornycroft.

None of his friends had arrived to claim him. It would have been remarkable, perhaps, if they had, since they had not been written to. Of male relatives he had none living, so far as was believed. His sister Susan was in a remote district of Yorkshire, and it was a positive fact that her address was unknown to both Anna Chester and Miss Thornycroft. Of course, the Miss Jupps could have supplied it on application, but nobody did apply. His half-sister, Mrs. Chester, was also uncertain in her domicile, here to-day, there to-morrow, and Anna had not heard from her for some months. The old saying that "Where there's a will there's a way," might have been exemplified, no doubt, in this case; but here there was no *will*. To all at Coastdown interested in the unfortunate matter, it had been a blessed relief could they have heard that Robert Hunter would lie in his quiet grave unclaimed for ever, his miserable end not inquired into. Richard Thornycroft had only too good personal cause to hope this, his sister also for his sake; and Mr. Thornycroft, acting on the caution Richard gave him as to the desirability of keeping other things quiet that were done on that eventful night, tacitly acquiesced in the silence. And Anna Chester—the only one besides who could be supposed to hold interest in the deceased —shuddered at the bare idea of writing to make it known; rather would she have cut off her right hand.

"They will be coming down fast enough with their inquiries from his office in London, when they find he does not return," spoke Richard gloomily the evening previous to the funeral. "No need to send them word before that time."

It was a snowy day. Mary Anne Thornycroft stood at the corridor window, from which a view of the path crossing from the village to the churchyard, could be obtained. Only for a few yards of it; but she watched carefully, and saw the funeral go winding past. The sky was clear at the moment; the snow had ceased; but the whole landscape, far and near, presented a sheet of white, contrasting strangely with the sombre black of the procession. Such a thing as a hearse was not known in Coastdown, and the body was carried by eight bearers. The clergyman, Mr. Southall, walked first, in his surplice—it was the custom of the place—having gone down to the Mermaid with the rest. Following it were Justice Thornycroft and his son Isaac, Captain Copp and Mr. Kyne, who acted as mourners; and a number of spectators brought up the rear. Richard had gone out to a distance that day; he had business, he said. Cyril had not been heard of. Mr. Thornycroft bore the expenses of the funeral. Some money had been found in the pockets of the deceased, a sovereign in gold and

some silver; nothing else except a white handkerchief.

Mary Anne strained her eyes, blinded by their
tears, upon the short line, as its features came
into view one by one, more distinctly than could
have happened at any time but this of snow. All
she had cared for in life was being carried past
there; henceforth the world would be a miserable
blank.   Dead!   Killed!   Murdered!—murdered
by her brother, Richard Thornycroft!   Had it
been done by anybody not connected with her by
blood, some satisfaction might have been derived
by bringing the crime home to its perpetrator.
Had it been brought home to Richard—and of
course *she* could not move to bring it—he would
have battled it out, persisting he was justified.
He called it justifiable homicide; she called it
murder.

The distant line of black has passed now, and
colours follow : men and women, boys and girls;
displaying, if not all the tints of the rainbow,
the shades and hues, dirt included, that prevail
in the every-day attire of the great unwashed.
Mary Anne glided into her room, and sank down
on her knees in the darkest corner.

Some time after, when she thought they might

be coming home, for the mourners would return to the Red Court, not the Mermaid, she came out again, her eyes swollen, and entered her step-mother's room. My lady, looking worse and worse, every day bringing her *palpably* nearer the grave, sat with her prayer-book in her hand. She had been reading the burial service. Ah, how changed she was; how changed in spirit!

"I suppose it is over," she said, in a subdued tone, as she laid the book down.

"Yes; by this time."

"May God rest his soul!" she breathed, to herself rather than to her companion.

Mary Anne covered her face with her hand, and for some moments there was perfect silence.

"I shall be going hence to-morrow, as you know," resumed Lady Ellis, "never to return, never perhaps to hold further communication with the Red Court Farm. I would ask you one thing first, Mary Anne, or the doubt and trouble will follow me: perhaps mix itself up with my thoughts in dying. What of Cyril?"

"Of Cyril?" returned Miss Thornycroft, lifting her face, rather in surprise. "We have not heard from him."

"Of course I know that. What I wish to ask is—what are the apprehensions?"

"There are none. Papa and my brothers seem perfectly at their ease in regard to him."

"Then whence arises this great weight of care, of tribulation, that lies on you?—that I can see lies on you, Mary Anne?"

"It is not on Cyril's account. The events of the last few days have frightened me," she hastened to add. "They have startled others as well as me."

"Ah, yes; true. And it seems to me so sad that you did not know the man who fired the pistol," continued Lady Ellis, who had no suspicion that Miss Thornycroft had not told the whole truth. "But to return to Cyril. If it be as you say, that they are easy about him, why, they must know something that I and others do not. I have asked your papa, but he only puts me off. Mary Anne, you might tell *me*."

Mary Anne made no immediate reply. She was considering what to do.

"The thought of Cyril is troubling me," resumed Lady Ellis. "As I lay awake last night, I thought *how much* I owed him. Were he my own son, his welfare could not be dearer to me

than it is. Surely, Mary Anne, whatever you
may know of him, I may share it. The secret—
if it be a secret—will be sacred with me."

"Yes, I am sure it will," spoke Mary Anne,
impulsively. "Not that it is any particular
secret," she added, with hesitation, framing the
communication cautiously; "but still, papa has
reasons for not wishing it to be known. He
thinks Cyril has gone to Holland."

"To Holland?"

"Yes; we have friends there. And a ship
was lying off here on Sunday night with other
friends on board. Some of them, subsequent to
the—the accident—came on shore in a little
boat, and papa and Richard feel quite certain
that Cyril went on board with them when they
returned. But there are reasons why this must
not be told to the public."

"What a relief!" cried the invalid. "My
dear, it is safe with me. Dear Cyril! he will
live to fulfil God's mission yet in the world. I
shall not see him for a last farewell here, but we
shall say it in heaven. Not a *farewell* there—a
happy greeting."

A sort of muffled sound downstairs, and Mary
Anne quitted the room to look. Yes, they were

coming in in their black cloaks and hatbands, having left Robert Hunter in the grave in St. Peter's churchyard.

For all that could be seen at present he seemed likely to lie there at rest, undisturbed, uninquired after. And the name of his slayer with him.

CHAPTER VI.

APRIL. And a fine spring evening.

The weeks have gone on since that miserable January time, bringing but little change to Coastdown or to those in it. Robert Hunter rested in his grave, uninquired for—though as to the word "rested" more hereafter—and Cyril Thornycroft had never returned. Lady Ellis had died in Cheltenham only a week after she went back to it.

That Cyril's remaining away so long and his not writing was singular in the extreme, no one doubted. Mr. Thornycroft grew uneasy, saying over and over again that some accident must have happened to him. Richard, however, had his private theory on the point, which he did not tell to the world. He believed now that Cyril and Hunter had returned that night together; that Cyril had witnessed the deliberate shot, had

put off to the ship, and in his condemnation of
the act would not come home to the Red Court
so long as he, Richard, was in it.

But Richard could not tell this to his father,
and Mr. Thornycroft one morning suddenly ordered
his son Isaac abroad—to France, to Holland, to
Flanders—to every place and town, in fact, where
there was the least probability of Cyril's being
found. The illicit business they had been engaged in caused them to have relations with
several places on the Continent, and Cyril might
be at any one of them. Isaac had but now returned—returned as he went, neither seeing nor
hearing aught of Cyril. It was beginning to be
more than singular. Surely if Cyril were within
postal bounds of communication with England,
he would write!

The supposition, held from the first, that he
had gone off in the smuggling boats to the ship
that night, and sailed with her on her homeward
voyage, was far more probable than it might
seem to strangers. Richard and Isaac had each
done the same, more than once; as, in his
younger days, had Mr. Thornycroft, thereby
causing no end of alarm to his wife. Cyril, it is
true, was quite different in disposition, not at all

given to wild rovings; but they had assumed the fact, and been easy. Richard, unwillingly, but with a view to ease her suspense, imparted the theory he had recently adopted to his sister; and she thought he might be right. As Mary Anne observed to her own heart, it was a miserable business altogether, looked at from any point.

No direct confidence had been reposed in Isaac. Richard shrank from it. Isaac had many estimable qualities, although he helped to cheat Her Majesty's revenue, and thought it glorious fun. But he could not avoid entertaining suspicions of his brother, and one day he asked a question. " Never mind," shortly replied Richard; " Hunter got his deserts." It was no direct avowal, but Isaac drew his own conclusions, and was awfully shocked. He was as different from Richard in mind, in disposition, in the view he took of things in general, as light is from dark. The blow to Isaac was dreadful. He could not, so to say, lift up his head from it; it lay on him like an incubus. *Now*, the coldness with which Anna had ever since treated him was explained, satisfactorily enough to his own mind. As a murderer's brother, her avoidance

of him was only natural. No doubt she was
overwhelmed with horror at being tied to him.
If he could but have divined that she suspected
him ! But they were all going in for mistakes ;
Isaac amongst the rest.

As if the real sorrow, the never-ceasing appre-
hension under which some of them lived, were
not enough to bear, rumours were about to arise
of an unreal one.

On this evening, in early April, Miss Thornycroft was alone. As she paced her parlour, in
the stately mourning robes of black silk and
crape, ostensibly worn for her stepmother, the
blight that had fallen on her spirit and her heart
might be traced in her countenance. The untimely and dreadful fate of Robert Hunter, to
whom she had been so passionately attached,
was ever present to her ; the false part she had
played at the inquest reddened her brow with
shame ; the guilt of her brother Richard haunted
her dreams. She would start up in fright from
sleep, seeing the officers of justice coming to
apprehend him; she would fancy sometimes she
saw her *father* taken, preparatory to the illicit
practices he had carried on being investigated
before a criminal tribunal. Mingling with this

—worse, if possible, than the rest—was the keenest weight of self-reproach.   She could not hide from herself, and no longer tried to do it, that her own deliberate disobedience had brought it all about—all, all!   But for flying in the face of her father's express commands, in not stopping the visit of Robert Hunter, he had been living now, and Richard's hand guiltless.

All this was telling upon Mary Anne Thorny-croft.   You would scarcely know her, pacing the lonely drawing-room, pale and sad, for the blooming, high-spirited, haughty girl of two months before.   Her father and Richard had gone to London on business, Isaac was out, she knew not where, and she was alone.   Her thoughts were dwelling on that fatal night—when were they ever absent from it?—and were becoming, as they sometimes did, unbearable. A nervous feeling came creeping over her; it had done so at times of late, fearless though she was by nature : a horror of being alone ; a dread of her own lonely self ; of the lonely room and its two candles ; an imperative demand for com-panionship.   She opened the door, and glided across the hall and lighted passages to the kitchen, framing an excuse as she went.

" Sinnett, will you—where's Sinnett ?"

The maids, three of whom were present, stood up at her entrance. They had been seated at the table making household linen.

" Sinnett is upstairs, miss. Shall I call her ?"

" No; she will be down directly, I dare say. I'll wait."

At that moment a sort of wild noise, half shriek, half howl, long-continued and ever-recurring, arose from without—at a distance, as yet. Mary Anne Thornycroft turned her ear to listen, her face blanching with dread fear; the least thing was sufficient to excite fear now.

The sounds approached nearer : they seemed to come from one in the very extremity of terror, and just then Sinnett entered the kitchen. Perhaps it has not been forgotten that the windows, of modern date, looked on the side walk, and thence towards the church and village. The shutters were not yet closed, the blinds not drawn down. In another instant, as the frightened women stood together in a group, one window was flung up, and a form propelled itself in, smashing a pane of glass. It proved to be Joe, the carter's boy; a sensitive, delicate lad, who had recently lost his mother, and was a favourite at the Red Court Farm. He lay for a moment amidst the shivers of glass, then rose up and clasped tight hold of Sinnett, his white face and shivering frame betokening some extraordinary cause of terror.

They put him in a chair, and held him there, he clinging to them. Miss Thornycroft authoritatively stopped all questions until he should be calmer. Sinnett brought him some wine, and the boy tried to sip it; but he could not keep his teeth still, and *he bit a piece out of the glass.* He looked over his shoulder at the window perpetually in ghastly fear, so one of the servants closed and barred the shutters. By degrees, he brought out that he had " seen a ghost."

Ghosts were rather favourite appendages to Coastdown, as we have read. They were not less implicitly believed in by the lower classes (not to bring in others) than they used to be, so the maids screamed and drew nearer Joe. This ghost, however, was not the old ghost of the plateau; as the boy is explaining, sobbing between whiles; but—Robert Hunter's.

" Nonsense !" reproved Sinnett. " Don't you be a coward, Joe, but just speak up and tell your tale sensibly. Come !"

"I went for the newspaper to Captain Copp's, as sent," answered the boy, doing his best to obey. "Mrs. Copp couldn't find it, and thought the captain had took it in his pocket to the Mermaid. Coming back here to say so, I see a figure in the churchyard hiding, like, behind a tombstone. I thought it were old Parkes, a-taking the short cut over the graves to his home, and I stood and looked at him. Then, as he rose himself a bit higher, I see him out and out. It were Mr. Hunter, with his own face and his own coat on—that black and white thing."

"His own coat!"

"It were," groaned the lad. "I never were thinking of anybody but Parkes, but when I once saw the coat and the face, I see it were Mr. Hunter."

Joe's hearers did not know what to make of this. Miss Thornycroft privately thought she must fall in a fit, too, she felt so sick and ill.

"Was the face—" began one of the maids, and stopped. Remembering Miss Thornycroft's presence, she substituted another word for the one she had been about to speak. "Was the face *red?*"

"No. White. It—"

At this juncture there came a sharp knock at
the window, as if the ghost were knocking to
come in. The boy howled, the women shrieked ;
and the ghost knocked again.

"Who's there?" called out Sinnett through
the shutters.

"It's me," answered a voice, which they recognised for that of Sarah Ford. "Is the
kitchen a-fire?"

Sinnett went to the entrance-door and called
to her to come in. On occasions, when pressed
for time, Sarah would give her messages at the
kitchen-window, to save going round. She had
brought the newspaper, one lent by the Red
Court to Captain Copp: Mrs. Copp had found it
after Joe's departure.

"He have seen a ghost," lucidly explained
one of the maids, pointing to Joe.

"Oh," said Sarah, who had a supreme con-
tempt for such things, regarding them as vanities,
akin to hysterics and smelling salts.

"I see it in the churchyard, close again his
own grave," said the boy, looking helplessly at
Sarah.

"See a old cow," responded she, emphatically.

"That's more likely. They strays in some-times."

"It were Mr. Hunter's ghost," persisted Joe. "He wore that there fur coat, and he stared at me like anything. I see his eyes a-glaring."

"The boy has been dreaming," cried Sarah, pityingly, as she turned to Sinnett. "I should give him a good dose of Epsom salts."

Which prescription Joe by no means approved of. However, Sarah could not stay to see it enforced; and we must go out with her.

Her master had come in when she reached home. It was supper time, and she began to lay the cloth. Old Mrs. Copp was there: she had arrived the previous day (after spending the winter in London) on another long visit. Peering through her tortoiseshell spectacles at Sarah, she told her in her decisive way that she had been twice as long taking home the newspaper as she need have been.

"I know that," answered Sarah, with composure. "A fine commotion I found the Red Court in: the maids screeching fit to deafen you, and young Joe in convulsions. I thought the kitchen-chimbly must be a-fire, and they were trying whether noise would put it out."

The captain looked up at this.   He was in an
easy-chair at the corner of the hearth-rug, a
glass of rum-and-water on a small stand at his
elbow : old Mrs. Copp sat in front of the fire, her
feet on the fender ; Amy was putting things to
rights on a side-table near the sofa, and Anna
Chester sat back on a low stool in the shade on the
other side of the fire-place, a book on her knee,
which she was making believe to read.

" Was the chimney on fire ?" snapped Mrs.
Copp.

" Just as much as this is," answered Sarah,
making a rattle with the knives and forks. " Joe
was telling them he had just seen Robert Hunter's
ghost.   They screeched at that."

The captain burst into a laugh : he had no
more faith in ghosts than Sarah had. Sea-serpents
and mermaids were enough marvel for him. Anna
glanced up with a perceptible shudder.

" By the way," said Mrs. Copp, taking her feet
off the fender and turning round to speak, " I
should like to come to the bottom of that extraordinary business.   You slipped out of my
questioning this morning, Anna ; I hardly knew
how.   Who *was* the man that fired the pistol on
the plateau ?   As to saying you did not see him

properly, you may as well tell it to the moon.
My belief is you are screening him," concluded
shrewd Mrs. Copp, watching the poor girl's
gradually whitening face.

" If I thought that ; if I thought she could
screen him, I'd—I'd—send her back to Miss
Jupp's," roared Captain Copp, who was still very
sore in regard to the part his women-kind had
played in the transaction.   " Screen a land
murderer !"

Anna burst out crying.

" My impression is, that it was Cyril Thornycroft," resumed Mrs. Copp.   " If he had not got
something bad on his conscience why should he
run away, and keep away."

Sarah took up the word, putting a tray of
tumblers down to do it.   " He may have his
reasons for staying away, and nobody but himself know anything about them.   But truth's
truth, all the world over, and I'll stand to it.   I
don't care whether it was the King of England,
or whether it was old Nick—it was not Cyril
Thornycroft."

" She is right," nodded the captain.   " He'd
be the least likely in all Coastdown to rush on
to the plateau at night, armed like a pirate, and

shoot a man. It was no more Cyril Thornycroft did that than it was me, mother."

"But, Sarah, what about poor Joe and the ghost?" interposed her mistress gently, upon whom the tale had made an unpleasant impression.

"Some delusion of his, ma'am: as stands to reason. I don't believe the boy has been right since his mother died ; he has had nothing but a down, scared look about him. He is just the one to see a ghost, he is."

"Where did he see it?"

"In the churchyard, *he* says, with its fur coat on."

"Fur coat!" broke in Captain Copp, his face aglow with merriment. "He meant a white sheet."

"Ah, he made a mistake there," said Sarah. And it was really something laughable to see how she as well as her master (mocking sceptics !) enjoyed the ghost in their grim way. In the midst of it, who should come in but Isaac Thornycroft.

He had not been a frequent visitor of late, rather to the regret of the hospitable captain. Set at rest on the score of any surreptitious liking for him on Anna's part—for it was impossible not to note her continual avoidance of him now—the captain would have welcomed him always in his pride and pleasure. Isaac Thornycroft was a vast favourite of his, and this was only the second visit he had paid since his return from abroad. Isaac looked as if he would like to join in the merriment, utterly unconscious what the cause might be.

"It's the best joke I've heard this many a day," explained the captain. "Your boy up at the Red Court—that Joe."

"Yes," said Isaac, the corners of his mouth relaxing in sympathy with the sailor's. "Well?"

"He went flying through the air, bellowing enough to arouse the neighbourhood, and tumbled in at your kitchen window in a fit, saying he had seen Robert Hunter's ghost."

"Breaking the glass and setting the maids a-screeching like mad," put in Sarah. "He saw it in the churchyard, he says, in its fur coat."

A troubled expression passed across Isaac's countenance. Captain Copp, attempting to drink some rum-and-water while he laughed, began to choke.

"What absurd story can they be getting up?" cried Isaac, sternly. "Some rumour of this sort—that Hunter had been seen in the churchyard—was abroad yesterday."

"You never saw a boy in such a state of fright, sir," observed Sarah. "Whether he saw anything or nothing, he'll not get over it this many a week."

"Saw anything or nothing! What d'ye mean?" fiercely demanded Captain Copp, suspending his laughter for the moment. "What d'ye suppose he saw?"

"Not a ghost," independently retorted Sarah. "I'm not such a simpleton. But some ill-disposed fellow may have dressed himself up to frighten people."

"If so, he shall get his punishment," spoke Isaac Thornycroft, with the imperative authority of a magistrate's son.

Captain Copp broke into laughter still. He could not forget the joke; but somehow all inclination for merriment seemed to have gone out of Isaac. He sat silent and abstracted for a few minutes longer, and then took his leave, declining to partake of supper.

"Where's Miss Anna gone?" cried the Captain to Sarah, suddenly missing her. "Tell her we are waiting."

Isaac lingered unseen in the little hall until she appeared, and took her hand in silence.

"Anna, this——"

But she contrived to twist it from him and turned to the parlour. He drew her forcibly to him, speaking in a whisper.

"Are you going to visit upon me for ever the work of that miserable night?"

"Hush! they will hear you."

But there was no other answer. Her face grew white, her lips dry and trembling.

"Don't you know that you are my wife?"

"Oh, heaven, yes! I would rather have died. I would die now to undo that night's work."

She seemed bewildered, as if unconscious of her words; but there was always the struggle to get from him. Had he been an ogre who might eat her, she could not have evinced more terror. Sarah opened the kitchen door, and Anna took the opportunity to escape. Isaac looked after her. If ever misery, horror, despair, were depicted on a human countenance, they were on Anna's.

"I did not think she was one to take it up like this," he said, as he let himself out. And in the tone of his voice, despairing as her face, there was a perfectly hopeless sound, as if he felt that he could not combat fate.

By the next day the story of the ghost, singular to say, had spread all over Coastdown; singular, because the report did not come from Joe, or from any of Joe's hearers. It appeared that a young fellow of the name of Bartlet, a carpenter's apprentice, in passing the churchyard soon after poor Joe must have passed it, saw the same figure, which he protested—and went straight to the Mermaid and protested—was that of Mr. Hunter. He was a daring lad of sixteen, as hardy as Joe was timid. The company at the Mermaid accused him of having got frightened and fancied it; he answered that he feared "neither ghost nor devil," and persisted in his story with so much cool equanimity, that his adversaries were staggered.

"It is well known that the ghosts of murdered people have been seen to walk," decided Mrs. Pettipher, the landlady, "and that of poor Mr. Hunter may be there. But as to the fur-coat, that can't be. It must have been a optical delusion of yours, Tom Bartlet. The coat's here; we have held possession of it since the inquest; for the ghost to have it on in the churchyard is a moral impossibility."

"I'll never speak again if it hadn't got the coat upon it," loudly persisted young Bartlet. "But for that white coat, staring out in the moonlight, I might never have turned my head to the churchyard."

"Had it got that there black fur down it, Tom?" demanded a gentleman, taking his long pipe from his mouth to speak.

"In course it had. I tell ye it was *the coat*, talk as you will."

This was the tale that spread in Coastdown. When the additional testimony of Joe and the maids at the Red Court Farm came to be added to it, something like fear took possession of three-parts of the community. The ghost of the plateau, so long believed in, was more a tradition than a ghost, after all; latterly, at any rate, nobody had been frightened by it; but this spirit haunting the churchyard was real —at least in one sense of the word. An uncomfortable feeling set in. And when in the course of a day or two other witnesses saw it, or pro-

fessed to see it, people began to object to go
abroad after nightfall in the direction of the
churchyard. A young man in the telegraph
office at Jutpoint brought over a message for
Isaac Thornycroft. He was a stranger to Coastdown, and had to inquire his way to the Red
Court Farm : misunderstanding the direction, he
took at first the wrong turning, which brought
him to the churchyard. Afterwards, the despatch
at length delivered, he turned into the Mermaid for a glass of ale, saying incidentally, not
in any fear, he had seen "sum'at" in the churchyard, a queer fellow that seemed to be dodging
about behind the upright gravestones. He had
never seen or heard of Robert Hunter; he knew
nothing of the report of the ghost ; but his de-
scription of the "sum'at" tallied so exactly with
the appearance expected, and especially with the
remarkable coat, that no doubt remained. Upon
which some ten spirits, well warmed with brandy-
and-water, started off arm-in-arm to the churchyard, there and then—and saw nothing for their
pains but the tombstones. Captain Copp heard
of the expedition, and went into a storm of indignation at grown men showing themselves to be
so credulous.

" Go out to a churchyard to look for a ghost !
Serve 'em right to put 'em into irons till their
senses come to 'em !"

Thus another day or two passed on, Mr.
Thornycroft and Richard being still absent from
home. Fears were magnified; fermentation increased; for, according to popular report, the
spirit of Robert Hunter appeared nightly in St.
Peter's churchyard.

CHAPTER VII.

It was a gusty night; the wind violently high even for the seaside; and Miss Thornycroft sat over the fire in her own sitting-room, listening to it as it whirled round the house and went booming away over the waste of waters.

Anna Chester was with her. Anna had shunned the Red Court of late; but she could not always refuse Miss Thornycroft's invitations without attracting notice; and she had heard that Isaac was to be away from home that day.

They had spent the hours unhappily. Heavy at heart, pale in countenance, subdued in spirit, it seemed to each that nothing in the world could bring pleasure again. Anna was altered just as much as Miss Thornycroft; worn, thin, haggard-eyed. Captain Copp's wife, seeing the change in Anna, and knowing nothing of the real cause, set it down to one that must inevitably bring discovery of the marriage in its train, and was fretting herself into fiddle-strings. Dinner was over; tea was taken; the evening went on. Quite unexpectedly Mr. Thornycroft and his eldest son arrived; Anna saw also, to her dismay, that Isaac was in; but none of them approached the sitting-room. Hyde, coming in later to replenish the fire, said the justice was not very well, and had retired to rest; Mr. Richard and Mr. Isaac had gone out. And the two girls sat on together, almost hearing the beating of each other's hearts.

"I wonder if the ghost is abroad this windy night!" exclaimed Anna, as a wild gust dashed against the windows and shook the frames.

"Don't joke about that, Anna," said Miss Thornycroft, sharply.

Anna looked round in surprise: nothing had been further from her thoughts than to joke; and indeed she did not know why she said it. "Of course the report is a very foolish one," she resumed. "I cannot think how any people can profess to believe it."

"Isaac saw it last night," said Mary Anne, quietly.

"Nonsense!" cried Anna.

" Ah! so I have answered when others said
they saw it. But Isaac is cool and practical ;
entirely without superstition ; the very last man I
know, save perhaps Richard, to be led away by fear
or fancy. He was passing the churchyard when
he saw—if not Robert Hunter, some one dressed
up to personate him ; but the features were
Robert Hunter's features, Isaac says ; they were
for a moment as distinct as ever he had seen
them in life."

" Did he tell you this ?"

" Yes."

" Could he have been deceived by his imagina-
tion ?"

" I think not. When a cool, collected man,
like my brother Isaac, dispassionately asserts
such a thing, in addition to the terrified asser-
tions of others, I at least believe that there must
be some dreadful mystery abroad, supernatural or
otherwise."

" A mystery ?"

" Yes, a mystery. Putting aside all questions
of the figure, how is it that the *coat* can appear
in the churchyard, when it remains all the while
in safe custody at the Mermaid ? "

Anna sat down, overwhelmed with the confu-

sion of ideas that presented themselves. The
chief one that struggled upwards was—how
should she ever have courage to pass the churchyard that night?

"Mary Anne! why did he not speak to
it?"

"Because some people came up at the time,
and prevented it. When he looked again the
figure was gone."

Precisely so. All this, just as Mary Anne
described it, had happened to Isaac Thornycroft
on the previous night. Robert Hunter, the hat
drawn low on his pale face, the unmistakeable
coat buttoned round him, had stood there in the
churchyard, looking just as he had looked in
life. To say that Isaac was not staggered would
be wrong—he was—but he recovered himself
almost instantly, and was about to call out to the
figure, when Mr. Kyne came past with young
Connaught, and stopped him. Isaac and his
family had to guard against certain discoveries
yet; and in the presence of the superintendent
of the coastguard, whose suspicions were already
too rife, he did not choose to proceed to investiga-
tion.

Silence supervened. The young ladies sat on

over the fire, each occupied with her sad and
secret thoughts.   The time-piece struck half-past
eight.

"What can have become of Sarah?" exclaimed Anna.   "Mrs. Copp was not well, and
my Aunt Amy said she should send for me
early."

Scarcely had the words left her lips, when that
respectable personage entered head foremost.
Giving the door a bang, she sank into an arm-
chair.   Anna stood up in wonder; Miss Thornycroft looked round.

"You may well stare, young ladies, but I can't
stand upon no forms nor ceremonies just now.
I don't know whether my senses is here or yonder,
and I made bold to come in at the hall door, as
being the nearest, and make straight for here.
There's the ghost at this blessed moment in the
churchyard."

Anna, with a faint cry, drew near to Miss
Thornycroft, and touched her for company.   The
latter spoke.

"Your fancy must have deceived you, Sarah."

"If anything has deceived me, it's my eyes,"
returned Sarah, really too much put out to stand
on any sort of ceremony whether in speech or

action—" which is what they never did yet,
Miss Thornycroft. When it struck eight my
mistress told me to go for Miss Chester. I thought
I'd finish my ironing first, which took me another
quarter of an hour; and then I put my blanket
and things away to come. Just as I was opening the house door I heard the master's voice
singing out for me, and went into the parlour.
' Is it coals, sir ?' I asked. ' No, it's not coals,'
says he; and I saw by his mouth he was after
some nonsense. ' It's to tell you to take care of
the ghost.' ' Oh, bran the ghost,' says I ; ' I
should give it a knock if it come anigh me.' And
so I should, young ladies."

"Go on, go on," cried Mary Anne Thornycroft.

"I come right on to the churchyard, and
what we had been saying made me turn my
eyes to it as I passed. Young ladies," she continued, drawing the chair closer, and dropping
her voice to a low, mysterious key, " if you'll
believe me, there stood Robert Hunter. He was
close by that big tombstone of old Marley's, not
three yards from his own grave !"

Mary Anne Thornycroft seemed unwilling to
admit belief in this, in spite of what she had her-

self been relating to Miss Chester. " Rely upon it, Sarah, your fears deceived you."

" Miss, I hadn't got any fears; at any rate, not before I saw him. There he was: his features as plain as ever they'd need be, and that uncommon coat on, which I'm sure was never made for anybody but a Guy Fawkes."

" Were you frightened then ?"

" I was not frightened, so to say, but I won't deny that I felt a creepishness in my skin; and I'd have given half-a-crown out of my pocket to see any human creature come up to bear me company. I might have spoke to it if it had give me time: I don't know: but the moment it saw me it glided amid the gravestones, making for the back of the church. I made off too as fast as my legs would carry me, and come straight in here. I knew my tongue must let it out, and I thought it better for you to hear it than them timorous servants in the kitchen."

" Quite right," murmured Miss Thornycroft.

" I never did believe in ghosts,"resumed Sarah ; " never thought to do it, and I'm not going to begin now. But after to-night, I won't mock at the poor wretches that have been frightened by Robert Hunters."

What now was to be done? Anna Chester
would not attempt to go home and pass the
churchyard with no protector but Sarah. Hyde
was not to be found; and there seemed nothing
for it but to wait until Richard or Isaac
came in.

But neither came. Between nine and ten
Captain Copp made his appearance in hot anger,
shaking his stick and stamping his wooden leg
at Sarah.

Had the vile hussey taken up her gossiping
quarters at the Red Court Farm for the night?
Did she think——

"I could not get Miss Chester away," interposed Sarah, drowning the words. "The ghost
is in the churchyard. I saw it as I came past."

The sailor-captain was struck dumb. One of
his women-kind avow belief in a ghost? He had
seen a mermaid himself; which creatures were
known to exist; but ghosts were fabulous things,
fit for nothing but the fancies of marines. Any
sailor in *his* fo'castle that had confessed to seeing
ghosts, would have got a taste of the yardarm.
"Get your things on this minute," concluded the
captain, angrily, to Anna. "I'll teach you to
be afraid of rubbishing ghosts! And that vile

bumboat woman! coming here with such a tale!"

"It's my opinion ghosts *is* rubbish, and nothing better; for I don't see the good of 'em; but this was Robert Hunter's for all that," spoke the undaunted "bumboat-woman." "I saw his face and his eyes as plain as ever I see my own in the glass, and that precious white coat of his with the ugly fur upon it. Master, you can't say that I gave as much as half an ear to this talk before to-night."

"You credulous sea-serpent!" was the captain's retort. "And that same coat lying yet in the tallet at the Mermaid with the blood upon it, just as it was taken off the body! Ugh! fie upon you!"

"If there's apparitions of bodies, there may be apparitions of coats," reasoned Sarah, between whom and her choleric but good-hearted master there was always a fight for the last word. "If it hadn't been for knowing his face, I should say some ill-conditioned jester had borrowed the coat from the Mermaid and put it on."

Away pegged the captain in his rage, scarcely allowing himself to say good-night to Miss Thornycroft; and away went Sarah and Miss

Chester after him, as close as circumstances permitted.

As they neared the churchyard Anna ventured to lay hold of the captain's arm, and bent her head upon it, in spite of his mocking assurances that a parson's daughter ought to be on visiting terms with a churchyard ghost; trusting to him to guide her steps. The captain was deliberating, as he avowed afterwards, whether to guide her into the opposite ditch, believing that a ducking would be the best panacea for all ghostly fears; when Sarah, who was a step in the rear, leaped forward and clung violently to his blue coat-tails.

"There!" she cried in a shrill whisper, before the astonished gentleman could free his tails or give vent to proper indignation, "there it is again, behind old Marley's tomb! Now then, master, is that the coat, or is it not?"

The captain was surprised into turning his eyes to the churchyard; Anna also, as if impelled by some irresistible fascination. It was too true. Within a few yards of them, in the dim moonlight—for the cloudy moon gave but a feeble light—appeared the well-known form of the ill-fated Robert Hunter, the very man whose dead body Captain Copp had helped to lay in the grave, so far as having assisted as a mourner at his funeral.

The captain was taken considerably aback; had never been half so much so before an unexpected iceberg; his wooden leg dropped submissively down and his mouth flew open. He had the keen eye of a seaman, and he saw beyond doubt that the spirit before him was indeed that of Robert Hunter. Report ran in the village afterwards that the gallant captain would have made off, but could not rid himself from the grasp of his companions.

" Hallo ! you sir !" he called out presently, remembering that in that vile Sarah's presence his reputation for courage was at stake, but there was considerable deference, not to say timidity, in his tone, " what is it you want, appearing there like a figure-head ?"

The ghost, however, did not wait to answer; it had already disappeared, vanishing into air, or behind the tombstones. Captain Copp lost not a moment, but tore away faster than he had ever done since the acquisition of his wooden leg, Anna sobbing convulsively on his arm, and Sarah hanging on to his coat-tails. A minute afterwards they were joined by Isaac Thornycroft, coming at a sharp pace from the direction of the village.

"Take these screeching sea-gulls home for me," cried the sailor to Isaac. "I'll go down to the Mermaid, and with my own eyes see if the coat is there. Some land-lubber's playing a trick, and has borrowed Hunter's face and stole the coat to act it in."

"Spare yourself the trouble," rejoined Isaac. "I have come straight now from the Mermaid, and the coat is there. We have been looking at it but this instant. It is under the hay in the room over the stable, doubled up and stiff, having dried in the folds."

"I should like to keelhaul that ghost," cried the discomfited captain. "I'd rather have seen ten mermaids."

Isaac Thornycroft, with an imperative gesture, took Anna on his own arm, leaving the captain to peg on alone, with Sarah still in close proximity to the coat-tails. He did not say what he had been doing all the evening, or why he should have come up at that particular juncture.

Upon the return of Richard to the Red Court an hour or two earlier, Isaac drew him at once out of the house to impart to him this curious fact of Hunter's ghost—as Coastdown phrased it —making its appearance nightly in the church-yard. Truth to say, the affair was altogether puzzling Isaac, bringing him trouble also. He had seen it himself the previous evening. Who was it ? what did it want ? whence did it come ? That it wore Hunter's face and form was indisputable. What then was it ? His ghost ? —a kind of marvel which Isaac had never yet believed in,—or a man got up to personate him ? Of course what Isaac feared was, that it might lead to discovery of various matters connected with the past.

He imparted all this to Richard. Richard scorned the information at first, ridiculed the affair, would not believe in the fear. Isaac proposed that they should go together to the churchyard, conceal themselves behind a convenient tombstone, watch for the appearance, and pounce upon it. Richard mockingly refused ; if he went at all to the place he'd go by himself and deal with the " ghost" at leisure. At present he had business with Tomlett.

They went together to Tomlett's cottage, and sat there talking. The baker's boy came up on an errand ; and as Mrs. Tomlett answered the

door they heard him tell her that " the ghost was
then—then—in the churchyard, his face and his
coat awful white."

"The coat has been stolen from the Mermaid," spoke Richard in his decisive tones.

"That fact was easy to be ascertained," Isaac
answered. And, rising at once from his seat, he
went to the Mermaid there and then. Calling
Pettipher, they went up the ladder to the tallet,
and Isaac convinced himself that there the coat
lay, untouched, and in fact unusable. From
thence he went his way to the churchyard, intending to see what he could do with the ghost himself, and thus overtook Captain Copp and his party.

Nothing of this did he say to Anna. Leaving
the ghost for the time being, he went on to Captain Copp's. She held his arm, not daring to
let it go ; her mind in a state of extreme distress.
Trembling from head to food went she ; a sob
breaking from her now and again.

"What can it be looking for ?" burst from
her in her grief and perplexity. " For you ?"

For the thought, the fear that had been
beating its terrible refrain in her brain was, that
Robert Hunter's spirit, unable to rest, had come
to denounce his destroyer. Such tales had over

and over again been told in the world's history :
why should not this be but another to add to
them ?

"Anna !" answered Isaac in a tone of surprise
and remonstrance, "you cannot seriously believe
that it is Hunter's spirit. Why talk nonsense ?"

Which reply she looked upon as an evasive
one.

" Can you solve the mystery then ?" she asked.
" That thing in the churchyard wears as surely
Hunter's face and form as you wear yours or I
mine. It is not himself : he is dead and buried ;
what then is it ?"

" Not his ghost," spoke Isaac. Whether he,
the cool-headed, practical, worldly man, who
believed hitherto in ghosts just as much as he did
in fairies, felt perfectly sure himself upon the
point now, at least he deemed it right to insist
upon it to his wife.

No more was said. But for Captain Copp's
turning back to converse with Isaac (having in a
degree recovered his equanimity) he might have
striven to get an explanat icn v ˙l l :
and then.

" Come in, come in, and take a sup of brandy,"

cried the hospitable captain when they arrived at
his house. "That beast of a ghost!"

"Oh, Sarah, what can have kept you!" exclaimed the captain's wife, in as complaining a
tone as so gentle a woman could use. "I have
had everything to do myself; the gruel to make
for Mrs. Copp, the hot water to take upstairs;
the——"

"It is not my fault, ma'am," interrupted the
subdued Sarah, as she rubbed her shoes on the
mat. "Miss Chester was afraid to come home
with me alone. There's Robert Hunter in the
churchyard."

Amy Copp glanced at her husband, expecting
an explosion of wrath at the words. To her
surprise, the captain heard them in patient
silence, his face as meek as any lamb's.

"Bring some hot water, Sarah, and get out
the brandy," said he.

Mixing a stiff glass for himself, Isaac declining to take any, he passed another in silence to
Sarah. Anna had escaped upstairs : her usual
custom when Isaac was there.

"Much obliged, sir, but I don't care for
brandy," was Sarah's answer. "My courage is
coming back to me, master."

Amy looked from one to the other, not knowing what to make of either.   " Have you really
seen anything ?" she asked.

" Seen Hunter, coat and all," gravely replied
the captain.   " Shiver my wooden leg, if we've
not!   I say, mother," he called out, stumping to
the foot of the stairs.   " Mother !"

" What is it, Sam ?" called back Mrs. Copp,
who was beginning to undress, and had not yet
taken her remedies for the cold.

" Mother, you know that mermaid in the
Atlantic—the last voyage you went with us ?
You wouldn't believe that I saw it ; you've only
laughed at me ever since : well, I've seen the
ghost to-night; so don't you disbelieve me any
more."

Captain Copp returned to the parlour, and in
a minute his mother walked in after him.   She
wore black stockings, fur slippers, a petticoat
that came down to the calves of her legs ; a
woollen shawl, and an enormous night-cap.
Isaac Thornycroft smothered an inclination to
laugh, but Mrs. Copp stood with calm equanimity, regardless of the defects of her costume.

" What's that about the ghost, Sam ?"

" I saw it to-night, mother.   It stood near its

own grave in the churchyard. And I hope you won't go on at me about that mermaid, after this. It had got long bright green hair, as I've always said, and was combing it out."

" The ghost had ?"

" No, the mermaid. The ghost was Hunter's. It looked just as he'd used to look."

Mrs. Copp stood rubbing her nose, and thinking the captain's conversion a very sudden one.

" Is this a joke, Sam ?"

" A joke ! Why, mother, I tell ye I saw it. Ask Sarah. I called out to know what it wanted, and why it came; but it wouldn't answer me."

" Well, it's strange," observed Mrs. Copp. " Sam's a simpleton about mermaids, but I'd have backed him as to ghosts. But now: you may have observed perhaps, all of you, that I've not said a syllable to ridicule this ghost of poor dead Mr. Hunter, and I'll tell you why. Last June, in Liverpool, a friend of mine was sitting up with her father, who was ill, when her sister's spirit appeared to her. It was between twelve and one at night—twenty minutes to one, in fact, for there was a clock in the room, and she had looked at it only a minute before; the candle——"

"Oh, mother, don't; pray don't!" implored poor Amy Copp, going into a cold perspiration, for she held a firm belief in things supernatural. "This one ghost is enough for us without any more. I shall never like to go up to bed alone again."

"The candle gave as good as no light, for the snuff was a yard long a'most, with a cauliflower on the top," continued Mrs. Copp, who persisted in telling her tale, supremely indifferent to her daughter-in-law's fears and her own robes. "Emma Jenkins, that was her name, heard a rustle in the room; it seemed to come in at the door, which was put open for air, flutter across, and stir the bed-curtains. (Don't you be foolish, Amy!) Naturally, Emma Jenkins looked up, and there she saw her sister, who had died a year before. The figure seemed to give just a sigh and vanish. Now," said Mrs. Copp, applying the moral, "if that was a ghost, this may be."

"You always said, you know, mother, that you didn'i believe in ghosts."

"Neither did I, Sam. But Emma Jenkins is not one to be taken in by fancy; as stands to reason, considering that she has gone thirteen voyages with her husband, short and long. Sea-going people are not liable to see ghosts where there's no ghosts to see; they have got their wits about them, and keep their eyes open. What are you smiling at, Mr. Thornycroft? Mrs. Jenkins had taken a glass of brandy-and-water, perhaps? Well, I don't know; sitting up with the sick is cold work, especially when they are too far gone to have anything done for 'em. But she always liked rum best."

The story over, Captain Copp plunged into a full account of the night's adventures, enlarging on the questions he asked with the view of bringing the ghost to book, and what he would have done had it only stayed. Sarah gave *her* version of the sight, both in going and coming. Mrs. Copp, forgetting her cold, plunged into another story of a man who died at sea the first time she sailed with her husband, and the belief of the sailors that he haunted the ship all the while it lay in Calcutta harbour; all to the shivering horror of poor Amy Copp; and Isaac Thornycroft, waking up from his reverie by fits and starts, sat on until midnight, like a man in a miserable dream.

CHAPTER VIII.

MARY ANNE THORNYCROFT had remained at home in a state of mind bordering on distraction. Look where she would, there was no comfort. Surely the death of Robert Hunter had been enough, with all its attendant dreadful circumstances, without this fresh rumour of his " coming again !"   Like Mrs. Copp, until impressed with her friend Emma Jenkins's experiences, Miss Thornycroft had never put faith in ghosts. She was accustomed to ridicule those who believed in the one said to haunt the plateau; but her scepticism was shaken now.

She had paid little attention to the first reports, for she knew how prone the ignorant are in general, and Coastdown in particular, to spread supernatural tales.   But these reports grew and magnified. Robert Hunter was dead and buried : how then reconcile that fact with this myste-

rious appearance said to haunt the churchyard?
Her mind became shaken; and when, on the
previous night, her brother Isaac imparted to her
the fact that he had seen it with his own sensible,
dispassionate eyes, a sickening conviction flashed
over her that it was indeed Robert Hunter's
spirit.   And now, to confirm it, came the testimony of the matter-of-fact Sarah.   Possibly, but
for the sad manner in which her nerves had been
shaken, this new view might not have been taken
up.

"What does it want?" she asked herself,
sitting there alone in the gloomy parlour: and
certain words just spoken by Sarah recurred to
her, as if in answer.   "It may want to denounce
its murderer."   Stronger even than the grief and
regret she felt at his untimely fate, at the abrupt
termination of her unhappy love, was the lively
dread of discovery, for Richard's sake.   *That*
must be guarded against, if it were possible; for
what might it not bring in its train?   The betrayal of the illicit practices the Red Court Farm
had lived by; the dishonour of her father and
his house; perhaps the trial—condemnation—
execution of Richard.

Sick, trembling, half mad with these reflections, pacing the room in agony, was she, when Richard entered. Had *he* seen the ghost? He looked as if he had. His damp hair hung about in a black mass, and his face and lips were as ghastly as Hunter's. His sister gazed at him with surprise : the always self-possessed Richard !

"Have you come from the village?" she asked.

"From that way."

"Did you happen to turn to the church-yard ?"

"Yes," was the laconic reply.

"You know what they say : that *his* spirit appears there."

"I have seen it," was Richard's unexpected answer.

Miss Thornycroft started. "Oh, Richard ! When ?"

"Now. I went to look, and I saw it. There's no mistake about its being Hunter, or some fool made up to personate him."

"It has taken away your colour, Richard."

Richard Thornycroft did not reply. He sat with his elbow on his knee, and his chin resting on his hand, looking into the fire. The once brave man, brave to recklessness, had been scared for the first time in his mortal life. The crime lying heavily on his soul had made a coward of him.

He said nothing of the details, but they must be supplied. Shortly after Isaac had quitted Tomlett's, Richard also left, intending to go straight home. As he struck across to the direct road—not the one by the plateau—a thought came to him to take a look at the churchyard; and he turned to it.

There was Robert Hunter. As Richard's footsteps sounded on the night air, nearing the churchyard, the head and shoulders of the haunting spirit appeared, raising themselves behind old Marley's high tombstone. Richard stood still. "There was no mistake," as he observed to his sister, "that it was Hunter." And the eyes of the two were strained, the one on the other. Suddenly the ghost came into full view and advanced, and Richard Thornycroft turned and fled. An arrant coward he at that moment, alone with the ghost and his own awful conscience.

Whether the apparition would have pursued him; whether Richard would have gathered bravery enough to turn and face it, could never be known. The doctor's boy, having been to the

heath with old Connaught's physic, ran past shout-
ing and singing; " the whistling aloud to keep his
courage up," as Bloomfield (is it not?) so subtly
says, was not enough now for those who had to
pass the churchyard at Coastdown. The ghost
vanished, and Richard strode on to the Red Court
Farm.

But he did not tell of all this. Mary Anne,
who had been bending her head on the arm of
the sofa, suddenly rose, resolution in her face and
in her low, firm tone.

" Richard, if you accompany me for protection,
I will go and see this spirit. I will ask what it
wants. Let us go."

" You!" he somewhat contemptuously exclaimed.

" I will steel my nerves and heart to it. I
have been striving to do so for the last half hour.
Better for me to hold communion with it than
any one else, save you. You know why,
Richard."

" Tush!" he exclaimed. " Do nothing. You'd
faint by the way."

" It is necessary for the honour and safety of
—of—this house," she urged, not caring to speak
more pointedly, " that no stranger should hear

what it wants. I will go now. If I wait until
to-morrow my courage may fail. I *go*, Richard,
whether with you or alone. You are not
afraid?"

For answer, Richard rose, and they left the
room. In passing through the hall, Mary Anne
threw on her woollen shawl and garden-bonnet,
just as she had thrown them on the night of
Hunter's murder; and they started.

Not a word was spoken by either until they
reached the corner of the churchyard. The
high, thickset hedge, facing them as they advanced, prevented their seeing into it, but they
would soon come in front, where the shrubs
grew low behind the iron railings. Miss Thornycroft stopped.

"You stay here, Richard. I will go on
alone."

"No," he began, but she peremptorily interrupted him.

"I will have it so. If I am to go on with
this, I will be alone. You can keep me within
sight." And Richard acquiesced, despising himself for his cowardice, but unable to overcome it.
He could not—no, he *could* not face the man
whose life he had taken.

Mary Anne Thornycroft opened the gate and
went in. In his place (he seemed to have
specially appropriated to himself) behind old
Marley's tomb, stood Robert Hunter. *How* she
contrived to advance—contrived to face him and
keep her senses, Mary Anne Thornycroft could
never afterwards understand.

Is it of any use to go on mystifying you, my
reader? Perhaps from the first you have suspected the truth. Any way, it may be better to
solve the secret, for time is growing limited, as
it was solved that night to Mary Anne and
Richard Thornycroft. The ghost, prowling about
still, was looking out for Richard, its sole object
all along; but it was Robert Hunter himself
and not his ghost. For Robert Hunter was not
dead.

He had been in London all the while they
mourned him so, as much alive as any of his
mourners, quite unconscious that he was looked
upon as murdered, and that the county coroner
had held an inquest on his body. A week since,
he had come down from London to Coastdown,
had come in secret, not caring to show himself
in the neighbourhood, and not daring to show
himself openly to the Thornycrofts. He wanted

12—2

to obtain an interview with Mary Anne; but to want it was a great deal easier than to get it, in consequence of that extravagant and hasty oath imposed upon him by Richard. According to its terms, he must not write to any one of the inmates of the Red Court Farm; he must not enter it; he must not show himself at Coastdown; and he could only hit upon the plan of coming down en cachette, keeping himself close by day, and watching for Richard at night. Not a very brilliant scheme, but he could think of no better; and, singular perhaps to say, there was no bar to his *speaking* to Richard if he met him; if the spirit of the oath provided against that, the letter did not; and Robert Hunter's business was urgent. So he came down to Jutpoint, walked over at night, and took up his quarters in a lonely hut that he knew of behind the churchyard, inhabited by a superannuated fisherman, old Parkes. The aged fisherman, of dim sight and failing memory, did not know his guest; he was easily bribed not to tell of his sojourn; and the rumours of the ghost had not penetrated to him. In that hut Hunter lay by day, and watched from the churchyard by night, as being a likely spot to see Richard, who used often to pass and repass it on his way to and

from the heath, and an *unlikely* one to be seen and
recognised by the public. With that convenient
tomb of old Marley's to shelter behind whenever
footsteps approached, he did not fear. Unfortunately, it was necessary that he should look out
to see whether the footsteps were not Richard's;
and this looking out had brought about all the
terror. His retreating place, when people had
intruded into the churchyard, Isaac for one, was
under a shelving gravestone at the back of the
church, where none would think of looking. And
there he had been on the watch, never dreaming
that he was being mistaken for his own ghost, for
he knew nothing of his supposed murder.

In little more than half-a-dozen sentences
this was revealed to Mary Anne Thornycroft. It
was the last night that he could stay: and he
had resolved, in the fear of having to go back to
London with his errand unexecuted, to accost
any one of the Thornycroft family that might
approach him, although by so doing the oath
was infringed. As their voices were borne on
the night air to the ear of Richard, sufficient
evidence that Hunter was a living man, a load
fell from his heart. In the first blissful throb of
the discovery, the thought that surged through

him, turning darkness into light, was, " If he is
alive, I am no murderer." He ran forward,
gained the spot where they stood, grasped
Hunter's hand and well-nigh embraced him.
He, the cold, stern, undemonstrative Richard
Thornycroft! he, with all his dislike of Hunter!

Do you consider well what that joy must
be—relief from the supposed committed crime of
murder? The awful nightmare that has been
weighing us down : the sin that has been eating
away our heartstrings! Some of us may have
faintly experienced this in a vision during
sleep.

" I do not understand it, Hunter," whispered
Richard, his words taking a sobbing sound as
they burst from his heaving breast in the inten-
sity of his emotion. " It is like awaking from
some hideous dream. If I shot you down, how
is it that you are here ?"

" You never shot me down. Old Parkes has
been driving at some obscure tale about young
Hunter being shot from the heights; but I
treated it as a childish old man's fancies. Mary
Anne, too, is wearing mourning for me, she says,
though ostensibly put on for Lady Ellis, and
came here to have speech of my ghost. I

thought ghosts had gone out with the eighteenth century."

All three felt bewildered; idea after idea crowding on their minds: not one of them as yet clear or tangible. Mary Anne could not so soon overcome the shivering sensation that had been upon her, and caught hold of her brother's arm for support. There was much of explanation to be had yet.

" Let us go and sit down in the church porch," she said; "we shall be quiet there."

They walked round the narrow path towards it. It was on the side of the church facing the Red Court. The brother and sister placed themselves on one bench: Hunter opposite. The moonlight streamed upon them, but they were in no danger there of being observed by any chance passer-by; for the hedge skirting the ground on that side was high and thick.

" That night," began Richard, " after you had gone away, what brought you back again?"

" Back where?" asked Hunter.

" Back on the plateau. Watching the fellows from the boats."

" I was not there. I did not come back."

The assertion sounded like a false one in the

teeth of recollection. Mary Anne broke the silence, her low tone rather an impatient one.

"I *saw* you there, Robert—I and Anna Chester. We were coming up to speak to you, and got as far as the Round Tower——"

"What was worse, *I* saw you," hoarsely broke in Richard. "After what had passed between us, and your solemn oath to me, I felt shocked at your want of faith. I was maddened by your bad feeling, your obstinate determination to spy upon and betray us; and I stood by that same Round Tower and shot you down."

"I do not know what you are talking of," returned Robert Hunter. "I tell you I never came back; never for one moment. I got to Jutpoint by half-past ten or a quarter to eleven, so you may judge that I stepped out well."

"Did Cyril go there with you?"

"Cyril! Of course not. He left me soon after we passed the village. He only came as far as the wherry. I have been looking for Cyril while dodging about in this churchyard. I'd rather have seen him than you. He would not have been violent, you know, and would have carried you my message."

" We have never seen Cyril since that night," said Miss Thornycroft.

" Not seen Cyril !" echoed Hunter. " Where is he ?"

" But we are not uneasy about him," said Richard, dropping his voice. " At least, I am not. We expect he went off in the boats with the smugglers when they rowed back to the ship that night after the cargo was run. Indeed, we feel positive of it. My father once did the same, to the terror of my mother. I believe she had him advertised. Cyril is taking a tolerably long spell on the French coast; but I think I can account for that. He will come home now."

" Still you have not explained," resumed Hunter. " What gave rise to this report that I was shot down ?"

" Report !" cried Richard, vehemently, his new-found satisfaction beginning to fade, as sober re-collection returned to him. " Somebody was shot, if you were not. We had the coroner's inquest on him, and he lies buried in this churchyard as Robert Hunter."

" But the features could not have been mine," debated Hunter.

" The face was not recognisable ; but the head

and hair were yours, and the dress was yours— a black dinner suit; and—— By the way," broke off Richard, " what *is* this mystery ? This coat, which you appear now to have on, is at this moment in the stables at the Mermaid, and has been ever since the inquest."

Does the reader notice that one word of Richard Thornycroft's—" Appear ?" *Appear* to have on ! Was he still doubting whether the man before him could be real?

" Oh, this is Dr. Macpherson's," said Hunter, with a brief laugh. " They were fellow coats, you know, Mary Anne. You did not send me my own—at least, I never received it; and one cold day, when I happened to be there, the professor surreptitiously handed me his out of a lumber closet, glad to get rid of it, hoping madame would think it was stolen. She could not forget the grievance of his having bought them. Why did not mine come with the portmanteau ?"

More amazement, more puzzle, and Richard further at sea than ever.

" When you left that night, you had your coat with you, Hunter. I saw you put it on."

" But I found it an encumbrance. I had

taken more wine than usual. I had had other things to make me hot, and I did not relish the prospect of carrying it, whether on or off, for five or six miles. So I took it off when we got to the wherry, and begged Cyril to carry it back with him, and send it with the portmanteau the following morning."

A pause of thought; it seemed they were trying to realize the sense of the words. Suddenly Mary Anne started, gasped, and laid her face down on her brother's shoulder, with a sharp, low moan of pain. *He* leaned forward and stared at Hunter, a pitiable expression of dread on his countenance, as the moonlight fell on his ghastly face and strained-back lips.

"Cyril said he was glad of it, and put it on, for he had come out without one, and felt cold," continued Hunter, carelessly. "He has not been exposed to all weathers, as I have. It fitted him capitally."

A cry, shrill and wild as that which had broken from the dying man in his fall, now broke from Richard Thornycroft.

"Stop!" he shouted, in the desperation of anguish; "don't you see?"

"See what?" demanded the astonished Hunter.

" That I have murdered my brother !"

Alas ! alas ! As they sat gazing at each other
with terror-stricken faces, you might have heard
their hearts beat.   Poor Richard Thornycroft!
Had any awakening to horror been like unto
his !

"Murdered your brother?" slowly repeated
Hunter.

It was too true.   The unfortunate Cyril
Thornycroft, arrayed in Hunter's coat, had been
mistaken by them for him in the starlight, and
Richard had shot him dead.   In returning home
after parting with Hunter at the wherry, there
could be no doubt that he had gone straight to
the heights to see whether the work which had
been planned for that night with the smugglers
was being carried on, or whether the discovery
made by Hunter had checked it.   It was the
coat, the miserable coat, that had deceived them.
And there was the general resemblance they bore
to each other, as previously mentioned.   In
height, in figure, in hair, they might have been
taken for one another, and had been, even in
the daylight, during Hunter's stay at Coastdown.
But it was not all this that had led to the dreadful error—it was the fatal and conspicuous coat.

Everything had contributed to the delusion, before life and after death. The face might have been anybody's for all the signs of recognition left in it. They wore, and only they, each a black dress dinner-suit, and Cyril, in his forgetfulness, had put away his purse and watch. His money—he generally carried it so—was loose in his pockets: how were they to know that the same custom was not followed by Hunter? The white pocket-handkerchief happened to bear no mark, and his linen was not disturbed. Nothing was taken off him but his upper clothes, the coat and the above-said dinner-suit. It was an exceptional death, you see, not a pleasant one to handle, and they just put a shroud over the under clothes, and so buried him. But for that would have been seen on the shirt the full mark—" Cyril Thornycroft."

Who shall attempt to describe the silence of horror that fell on the church porch after the revelation? Richard quitted his seat and stood upright, looking out, as it seemed; and his sister's head then sought a leaning-place against the cold trellis-work.

" How was it you never wrote to me ?" at length asked Robert Hunter, in a low voice. " Had you done so, this mystery would have been cleared up."

"Wrote to *you?*" wailed Richard. "Do you forget we thought you were here?" stamping his foot on the sod of the churchyard.

"I can hardly understand it yet," mused Robert Hunter.

Richard Thornycroft turned and touched his sister. "Let us go home, Mary Anne. We have heard enough."

Without a word of dissent or approval, she rose and put her arm within Richard's; her face white and rigid as it had been at the coroner's inquest. Hunter spoke then.

"But, Mary Anne—what I wanted to say to you—I have not yet said a word of it."

"I cannot talk to-night," she shuddered. "I cannot—I cannot."

"Then—I suppose—I must stay another day," he rejoined, wondering privately what would be said and thought of him in London. "May I come to the Red Court to-morrow?"

"If you will," answered Richard. "No necessity for concealment now. I absolve you from your oath."

But Mary Anne saw further than either of

them; saw that it would not do. Richard walked forward, but she remained, and touched Mr. Hunter on the arm.

" No, Robert, it must not be. You must still be in this neighbourhood—for a time at any rate —as dead and buried."

" Why? Far better to let them know I have not been murdered : and set their suspicions at rest."

" That you have not, but that another has," she returned, resentfully. " Would you have them rake up the matter, and hold a second inquest, and so set them upon my unfortunate brother Richard? His punishment, as it is, will be sufficiently dreadful and lasting."

" Do not speak to me in that tone of reproach," was the pained rejoinder. " You may be sure that I deeply sympathize and grieve with you all. I will continue to conceal myself : but how shall I see you? One more day, and business will enforce my return to London."

" I will see you here, in this place, to-morrow night."

" At what hour ?"

" As soon as dusk comes on. Say seven."

" You will not fail, Mary Anne ?"

"Fail!" she repeated, vehemently. Then, in a quieter tone, as she would have walked away, "No; I will be sure to come."

Robert Hunter grasped her hand, as if to draw her towards him for a fond embrace, but Miss Thornycroft wrenched her hand away with a half cry, and went on to join her brother. "Good night, dear Robert," she presently called out, in a gentle voice, as if to atone for her abrupt movement: but oh! what a mine of anguish that voice betrayed!

In the midst of the same silence that they had come, they went back again, walking side by side in the road, but not touching each other. Ah! what anguish it was that lay on both of them! We never know; in great affliction we are so apt to think that we can bear nothing worse, and live. It had seemed to Richard Thornycroft and his sister, when they went down to the church-yard, that no heavier weight of misery could be theirs than that lying on them; it seemed now in going back, as if that had been light, compared with this.

"Richard," she whispered, in her great pity, as they passed through the entrance gates of the Red Court Farm, "he is better off; he was fit to go. You know it must be so. Cyril is in heaven with God ; it seems now as if he had been living on for it."

Richard hardly heard the words. He was thinking his own thoughts. " The death must have been a painless one."

She was true to her promise. The following evening, when dark fell and before the moon was up, Robert Hunter and Miss Thornycroft sat once more in the church porch. The night was very cold, sharp, raw ; but from a feeling of considerate delicacy, which she understood and mentally thanked him for, he was without a great-coat. He rightly judged that the only one he had with him could in her eyes be nothing but an object of horror.

What a day that had been at the Red Court! Mr. Thornycroft had sat on the magisterial bench at Jutpoint, trying petty offenders, unconscious that there was a greater offender at his own house demanding punishment. Richard Thornycroft felt inclined to proclaim the truth and deliver himself up to justice. The remorse which had taken possession of him was greater than he knew how to bear ; and it seemed that to expiate his offence at the criminal bar of his country, would be more tolerable than to let it thus prey upon him in silence, eating away his heart and his life. Consideration for his father and sister, for their honourable reputation, alone withheld him. He and Cyril had been fond brothers. Cyril, of delicate health and gentle manners, had been, as it were, the pet of the robust justice and his robust elder sons. The home, so far as Richard was concerned, must be broken up: he would go abroad, the farther distant the better. But for his sister, he had started that day. Something of this she told Mr. Hunter, in an outburst of her great suffering.

"Oh, Robert! even allowing that he shall escape, what a secret it will be for me and my brother Isaac to carry through life!"

"Time will soften it to you. You are both innocent."

"Time will never soften it to me. My dear brother Cyril!—so loving to us all, so *good!*"

Her hands were before her face, as if she would conceal its tribulation from the dark night. Robert Hunter, who had been standing, drew her hands within his, sat down beside her on the narrow bench, and kept them there.

"Time is wearing on, Mary Anne, and I must be at Jutpoint to-night. May I say what I came down from town to say? Though it pains me to enter upon it now you are in this grief."

"What is it, Robert?"

"You have not forgotten that there was a probability of my going abroad? Well, the arrangements are now concluded, and I start in the course of a few days. I did not think of being off before the summer, but it has been settled differently."

"Yes. Well?"

"This alters my position altogether in a pecuniary point of view, and I shall now rest at ease, the future assured. The climate is excellent; the residence out all that can be wished for. In a week from this I ought to take my departure."

"Yes," she repeated, in the same tone of apathy as before. "What else? Make haste, Robert—I must begone; I am beginning to shiver. I have these shivering fits often now."

"I want you to go with me, my love," he whispered, in an accent of deep tenderness. "I came down to urge it; but now that this unfortunate affair has been made known to me, I would doubly urge it. As my wife, you will forget——"

"Be quiet, Robert!" she impetuously interrupted, "you cannot know what you are saying."

"Yes, I do; I wish you to understand. I may be away for five years."

"So much the better. You and I, of all people in the world, must live apart. Was this what you had to say?"

"I thought you loved me," he rejoined, quite petrified at her words.

"I did love you; I do love you; if to avow it will do any good now. But this dreadful sorrow has placed a barrier between us."

There ensued a bitter pause. Robert Hunter was smarting with a sense of injustice.

"Mary Anne! Surely you are not laying on *me* the blame of that terrible calamity!"

"Listen, Robert," she returned. "I am not so unjust as to blame you for the actual calamity, but I cannot forget that you and I have been the cause of it."

"You!"

"Yes, I. When my father heard that I had invited you down, he came to me, and forbid me to let you come. I see now why. They did not want strangers in his house, who might see more than was expedient. He commanded me to write and stop you. I disobeyed; I thought papa spoke but in compliance with a whim of Richard's; and I would not write. Had I obeyed him, all this would have been spared. Again, when you and I told what the supervisor said, that there were smugglers abroad, my father ordered us, you especially, not to interfere. Had you observed his wishes to the letter, Cyril would have been alive now. These reflections haunt me continually; they will be mine for ever. No, Robert, you and I must live apart. If I were to marry you, I should expect Cyril to rise reproachfully before me on our wedding-day."

"Oh, Mary Anne! Believe me you see matters in a false light. If——"

"I will not discuss it," she peremptorily interrupted, "it would be of no avail, and I shudder while I speak. Spare me argument."

"I think you are forgetting that I have a stake in the matter as well as yourself," he quietly said, his tone proving how great the pain was. "Do you not know what, deprived of you, my future life will be? At least, I have a right to say a few words."

" Well—yes, that's true. I suppose I did forget, Robert."

"Forgive me then for reminding you that the sole and immediate cause of Cyril's death, is *Richard*. I did nothing whatever to help it on; my conscience is clear; the most prejudiced man could not charge me with it. And you? It is certainly a pity—I am speaking plainly—that you disobeyed Mr. Thornycroft in allowing me to come to the Red Court; it was very wrong; but still you did it not with any ill intention, and certainly do not merit the punishment of being condemned to live a lonely life."

" But Richard is my brother. See what it has brought on *him*."

" What he has brought upon himself," corrected Mr. Hunter. " I do not see that his being your brother throws, or should be allowed to throw any bar upon your marriage with me. You would not say so had he been a stranger."

" Where is the use of arguing?" she broke in. " I cannot bear it; I will not hear it. All is at an end between us. Do you forgive me, Robert, if I cause you pain? Nothing in the world, or out of it, shall ever induce me to become your wife."

" Is this your fixed determination ?"

" Fixed and unalterable. Fixed as those stars above us. Fixed as Cyril's grave."

" Then it only remains for me to return the way I came," he gloomily said. " And the sooner I start the better."

They stood up; looking for a moment each into the other's face. There was no relenting in hers.

" Fare you well, Mary Anne."

She put her hand into his, and, overcome by the dead anguish at her heart, burst into tears. He drew her to his breast. None can know what that anguish was to her, even of the parting. He held her to him and soothed her sobs, now with a loving look, now with a gentle action; and then he broke into words of passionate entreaty, that she would retract her cruel determination, and suffer him to speak to her father. But he little knew Mary Anne Thornycroft if he thought that she would yield.

" Say no more; it is quite useless. Oh, Robert, don't you see it is as bitter for me as for you ?"

" No; or you would not inflict it."

" Strive to forget me, Robert," she murmured.

" We have been very dear to each other, but you must find some one else now. Perhaps we may meet in after life—when you are a happy man with wife and children !"

He went with her to the churchyard gates, and watched her as she turned to her home. And so they parted. Robert Hunter retraced his steps up the churchyard, and from behind a gravestone, where he had laid them out of sight, took up his little black travelling-bag, and the rolled-up coat, the counterpart of which had proved so unlucky a coat for the Red Court Farm. He never intended to put it on again—at least in the neighbourhood of Coastdown. Then he set off to walk to Jutpoint, avoiding the road by means of a by-path, as he had set off to walk that guilty night some weeks before.

The night had clouded over, the stars disappeared, the moon was not seen. Drops of rain began to fall, threatening a heavy shower. On it came, thicker and faster; wetter and wetter got he; but it may be questioned whether he gave to it one single thought.

His reflections were buried quite as much in the past as in the present. He murmured to himself the word " RETRIBUTION." He asked

how *he* could ever have dreamt of indulging a
prospect of happiness; he almost laughed at the
utter mockery of the hope. As he had blighted
his wife's life, so had Mary Anne Thornycroft,
his late and only love, now blighted his. She—
poor Clara—had died of the pain ; he, of sterner
stuff, must carry it along with him. Amid his days
of labour, through his nights of perhaps broken
rest, it would lie upon him—a well-earned re-
compense! No murmur came forth from his
heart or lips; he simply bowed his head in ac-
knowledgment of the justice. God was ever true.
And Robert Hunter lifted his hat in the pouring
rain, and raised his eyes to heaven in sad thankfulness that the pain his sin had caused was at
length made clear to him.

CHAPTER IX.

But there's something yet to tell of the evening. It was getting towards dusk when Isaac Thornycroft went his way to Captain Copp's, intending boldly to ask Miss Chester to take a walk with him, should there be no chance of getting a minute with her alone at home.

The state in which he was living, touching his wife's estrangement (not their separation, that was a present necessity), was getting unbearable; and Isaac, who had hitherto shunned an explanation, came to the rather sudden resolution of seeking it. Although his brother had shot Robert Hunter, it could not be said to be a just reason for Anna's resenting it upon *him*. Not a syllable did Isaac yet know of the discovery that had taken place, or that Cyril was the one lying in the churchyard.

In the free and simple community of Coast-

down, doors were not kept closed, and people
entered at will. Rather, then, to Isaac's surprise,
as he turned the handle of Captain Copp's, he
found it was fastened, so that he could not enter.
At the same moment his eyes met his wife's, who
had come to the window to reconnoitre. There
was no help for it, and she had to go and let
him in.

"At home alone, Anna! Where are they all?
Where's Sarah?"

Anna explained: bare facts only, however, not
motives. It appeared that the gallant captain,
considerably lowered in his own estimation by the
events of the past night, and especially that he
should be so in the sight of his "womenkind,"
proposed a little jaunt that day to Jutpoint by
way of diverting their thoughts, and perhaps his
own, from the ghost and its reminiscences. His
mother—recovered from her incipient cold—she
was too strong-minded a woman for diseases to
seize upon heartily—agreed readily, as did his
wife. Not so Anna. She pleaded illness, and
begged to be left at home. It was indeed no
false plea, for her miserable state of mind was
beginning to tell upon her. They had been expected home in time for tea, and had not come.

Anna supposed they had contrived to miss the omnibus, which was in fact the case, and could not now return until late. How Mrs. Sam Copp would be brought by the churchyard was a thing easier wondered at than told. As to Sarah, she had but now stepped out on some necessary errands to the village.

In the satisfaction of finding the field undisturbed for the explanation he wished entered on, Isaac said nothing about his wife being left in the house alone, which he by no means approved of. It was not dark yet, only dusk : but Anna said something about getting lights.

"Not yet," said Isaac. "I want to talk to you; there's plenty of light for that."

She sat down on the sofa; trembling, frightened, sick. If her husband was the slayer of Robert Hunter—as she believed him to be—it was not agreeable to be in the solitary house with him; it was equally disagreeable to have to tell him to go out of it. Ah, but for that terrible belief, what a happy moment this snatch of intercourse might have been to them! this sole first chance for weeks and weeks of being alone, when they might speak together of future plans with a half-hour's freedom.

She took her seat on the sofa, scarcely conscious what she did in her sick perplexity. Isaac sat down by her, put his arm round her waist, and would have kissed her. But she drew to the other end of the large sofa with a gesture of evident avoidance, and burst into tears. So he got up and stood before her.

"Anna, this must end, one way or the other; it is what I came here to-night to say. The separated condition in which we first lived after our return was bad enough, but that was pleasant compared to what it afterwards became. It is some weeks now since you have allowed me barely to shake you by the hand; never if you could avoid it. Things cannot go on so."

She made no reply. Only sat there trembling and crying, her hands before her face.

"What have I done to you? Come, Anna, I must have an answer. What have I done to you?"

She spoke at last, looking up. In her habit of implicit obedience, there was no help for it; there could be none when the order came from *him*.

"Nothing——to me."

"To whom, then? What is it?"

"Nothing," was all she repeated.

"Nothing! Do you repent having married me?"

"I don't know."

The answer seemed to pain him.   He bent his handsome face a little towards her, pushing back impatiently his golden hair, as if the fair bright brow needed coolness.

"I thought you loved me, Anna?"

"And you know I did.   Oh, that is it!   The misery would be greater if I loved you less."

"Then why do you shun me?"

"Is there not a cause why I should?" she asked in a low tone, after a long pause.

"*I* think not.   Will you tell me what the cause may be?"

She glanced up at him, she looked down, she smoothed unconsciously the silk apron on which her nervous hands rested, but she could not answer.   Isaac saw it, and, bending nearer to her, he spoke in a whisper.

"Is it connected with that unhappy night—with what took place on the plateau?"

"I think you must have known all along that it is."

"And you consider it a sufficient reason for shunning me?"

" Yes, do not *you ?*"

" Certainly not."

Great though her misery was, passionately though she loved him still, the cool assertion angered her. It gave her a courage to speak that nothing else could have given.

" It was a dark crime; the worst crime that the world can know. Does it not lie on your conscience ?"

" No; I could not hinder it."

" Oh, Isaac! Had it been anything else; anything but *murder,* I could have borne it. How you can bear it, and live, I cannot understand."

" Why should I make another's sin mine? No one can deplore it as I do; but it is not my place to answer for it. I do not understand you, Anna."

She did not understand. What did his words mean ?

" Did you not kill Robert Hunter ?"

" *I* kill him! You are dreaming, Anna! I was not near the spot."

" Isaac! ISAAC ?"

" Child! have you been fearing *that ?*"

" For nothing else, for nothing else could I

have shunned you. Oh, Isaac! my dear husband, how could the mistake arise?"

"I know not. A mistake it was; I affirm it to you before God. I was not on the plateau at all that night."

He opened his arms, gravely smiling, and she passed into them with a great cry. Trembling, moaning, sobbing; Isaac thought she would have fainted. Placing her by his side on the sofa, he kept still, listening to what she had to say.

"As I looked out of the Round Tower in the starlight, I caught a momentary glimpse of—as I thought—you, and I saw the hand that held the pistol take aim and fire. I thought it *was* you, and I fainted. I have thought it ever since. Mary Anne, in a word or two that we spoke together, seemed to confirm it."

"Mary Anne knew it was not I. It is not in my nature to draw a pistol on any man. Surely, Anna, you might have trusted me better!"

"Oh, what a relief!" she murmured, "what a relief!" then, as a sudden thought seemed to strike her, she turned her face to his and spoke, her voice hushed.

"It must have been Richard. You are alike in figure."

" Upon that point we had better be silent," he answered, in quite a solemn tone. "It is a thing that we are not called upon to inquire into ; let us avoid it. I am innocent : will not that suffice ?"

" It will more than suffice for me," she answered. " Since that night I have been most wretched."

" You need not have feared me in any way, Anna," was the reply of Isaac Thornycroft. " Were it possible that my hand could become stained with the blood of a fellow-creature, I should hasten to separate from you quicker than you could from me. Whatever else such an unhappy man may covet, let him keep clear of wife and children."

" Forgive me, Isaac ! Forgive me !"

" I have not been exempt from the follies of young men, and I related to you the greater portion of my share of them, after we married," he whispered. " But of dark crime I am innocent —as innocent as you are."

" Oh, Isaac ! my husband, Isaac !"

He bent his face on hers, and she lay there quietly, her head nestling in his bosom. It seemed to her like a dream of heaven after the past; a very paradise.

" You will forgive me, won't you?" she softly breathed.

" My darling !"

But paradise cannot last for ever, as you all know ; and one of them at any rate found himself very far on this side it ere the night was much older. As Sarah let herself into the house with her back-door key, Isaac quitted it by the front, and bent his steps across the heath.

In passing the churchyard, he stood and looked well into it. But there was no sign of the ghost, and Isaac went on again. How little did he suspect that at that very selfsame moment the ghost was seated round in the church porch, in deep conversation with his sister ! Having an errand in the village, he struck across to it ; and on his final return home a little later, he was astonished to overtake his sister at the entrance gates of the Red Court Farm, her forehead pressed upon the ironwork, and she sobbing as if her heart would break.

" Mary Anne ! what is the matter ? What brings you here ?"

"Come with me," she briefly said. "If I do not tell some one, I shall die."

Walking swiftly to one of the benches on the lawn, she sat down on it, utterly indifferent to the rain that was beginning to fall. Isaac followed her wonderingly. Poor thing! the whole of the previous day and night she had really almost felt as if she should die—die from the weight of the fearful secret, and the want of some one to confide in. Richard was the only one who shared it, and she was debarred by pity from talking to him.

There, with the fatal plateau in front of him, and the rain coming down on their devoted heads, Isaac Thornycroft learnt the whole— learnt to his dismay, his grief, his horror, that the victim had been his much-loved brother Cyril; and that Robert Hunter was still in life.

He took his hat off, and wiped his brow; and then held his hat before his face, after the fashion of men going into church—held it for some minutes. Mary Anne in her own deep emotion did not notice his.

"Isaac, don't you pity me?"

"I pity us all."

14—2

" And there will be the making it known to
papa.   He must be told."

" Ay."

" Richard will leave Coastdown for ever.   He
could not remain in it, he says.   I am not com-
petent to advise him, Isaac.   You must."

" Richard has never yet taken any advice but
his own."

" Ah! but he is changed to-day.   He has
been changed a little since that dreadful night.
I suppose you have known all along that it was
Richard who—who did it?"

" Not from information : I saw that you knew ;
that you were in his confidence.   Of course I
could not help being sure in my own mind that
it must have been Richard.   I fancy"—he turned
and looked full at his sister—" that Miss Chester
thought it was I."

" Yes, I know she did," was the assured answer.   " It was better to let her think so.   Safer
for Richard, better for you."

" Why better for me?"

" Because—it is not a moment to be reticent,
Isaac—Anna Chester once appeared too much
inclined to like you.   That would never do, you
know."

He turned his head away; a soft remembrance parting his lips, a look of passionate love, meant for his absent wife, lighting his eyes.

" You will get wet sitting here, Mary Anne."

She arose, and they went indoors. Isaac was passing straight through to the less-used rooms when his sister stopped him.

Rooms that would never have been closed to the rest of the house, but for the smuggling practices so long carried on by the Thornycroft family. In the rooms themselves there was absolutely nothing that could have led to betrayal, or any reason why they might not have been open to all the household : but it was necessary to keep that part of the house closed always, except to Mr. Thornycroft and his sons, lest it should have been penetrated to at the few exceptional times when the cargo was being run, or the dog-cart laden subsequently with the spoil. When once the cargo was safely lodged in the cavern within the rocks, it might remain there in security to some convenient time for removing it. This was always done at night. Richard and Isaac Thornycroft, Tomlett and Hyde, brought up sufficient of the parcels to fill the dog-cart, which one of the

sons, sometimes both, would then drive away with
and deposit with Hopley, their agent at Dartfield, whose business it was to convey the booty to
its final destination. The next night more would
be taken away, and so on. Sometimes so large
was the trade done, so swift were the operations,
that one cargo would not be all sent away before
another was landed. At another period perhaps
three months elapsed and no boat came in.
With this frequent going out by night with the
dogcart, no wonder the young Thornycrofts got
the credit of being loose in their habits, and that
the justice encouraged the notion.

The sumptuous dinners at the Red Court Farm
(or suppers, according to the convenience and
time of year) were kept up as a sort of covering
to the illicit doings. When the gentlemen of the
neighbourhood, including the superintendent of
the coastguard, had their legs under the hospitable board, or the servants subsequently under
theirs in the kitchen, they could not be wander-
ing about out of doors, seeing inexpedient things.
It was not often of late years Mr. Thornycroft
aided in the run; he left it to Richard and Isaac,
and stayed with his guests. On the night Lady
Ellis saw him he had gone out, found there was

a sea fog, and came in again; denying it afterwards to her (as faithful Hyde had done) lest she
should next question why he changed his coat and
put on leggings.

The late superintendent, Mr. Dangerfield, had
allowed rule to get lax altogether, but he had, of
course, a certain amount of watching kept up.
On the occasion of a dinner or supper at the
Red Court (always given when a cargo was waiting to be run), Mr. Dangerfield would contrive
to let his men know that he was going to it; as
a matter of fact, not a man troubled himself to go
near the plateau that night; the Mermaid had
them instead; and all too often it happened that
one of the young Mr. Thornycrofts would go in
and stand treat. No fear of the men's stirring
any more than their master. But from the fact
of the Half-moon beach being visible only from
the plateau, and for the supernatural tales connected with the latter, they had never escaped
being seen so long as they did.

The ghostly stories—not of Robert Hunter—
had done more than all to prevent discovery. It
could not be said that the Thornycrofts raised
them in the first place; they did not; but when
they perceived how valuable an adjunct they

were likely to prove, they took care to keep them up. Report went that the late Mrs. Thornycroft had died from the fears induced by superstition. It was as well to keep up that belief also; but she had died from nothing of the sort. What she had really died of—so to say—was the smuggling. When the discovery came to her at first, through an accident, of the practices carried on by her husband and sons—as they had been by her husband's brother and his father before him—it brought a great shock. A timid, right-minded, refined woman, the dread of discovery was perpetually upon her afterwards; she lived in a state of inward fear night and day; and this most probably induced the disorder of which she died —a weakness that got gradually worse and worse, and ended in death. When she was dying, not before, she told them it had killed her. Had Mr Thornycroft known of it earlier, he might have given it up for her sake, for he was a fond husband. But he had not known of it; and her death and its unhappy cause left upon them a great sorrow: one that could not be put away. The same grief at the practices, and dread of what a persistence in them might bring forth, had likewise lain on Cyril, and been the secret of his declining to take Orders so long as they should be carried on. Mr. Thornycroft himself was getting somewhat tired of it, as he told Cyril; he had made plenty of money, but Richard would not hear of their being given up.

Perhaps from habit more than anything else, Isaac was passing on to the back rooms, but Mary Anne arrested him. "Stay with me a little while, Isaac; you do not know how lonely it is for me now."

He acquiesced at once. He was ever good-natured and kind, and they turned into the sitting-room, she calling a servant to take her shawl and bonnet. Not empty, as she had anti-cipated, was the parlour, for Richard was there.

"I have told Isaac all," said Mary Anne, briefly. And Isaac, in his great compassion, went up to his brother and laid his hand on him kindly.

Poor Richard Thornycroft! His eyes hollow, his brow fevered, his hands burning, he paced there still in his terrible remorse. A consuming fire had set in, to prey upon him for all time. He spoke a few disjointed words to Isaac, as if in extenuation.

"I felt half maddened at Hunter's duplicity of conduct that night. I had warned him that I would shoot him if he went again on the plateau, and I thought I was justified in doing so. *Why* did Cyril put the coat on?"

"Let this be a consolation to you, Richard— that you did not intend to harm your brother," was all the comfort Isaac could give.

"Had it been any one but my brother! had it been any but my brother!" was the wailing answer. "The curse of Cain rests upon me."

Walking about still in his restlessness as he said it! He had never sat, or lain, or rested since leaving the churchyard the previous night, but paced about as one in the very depths of despair. Mary Anne slipped the bolt of the door, and they began to consult as to the future. At this dread consultation, every word of which will linger in the remembrance of the three during life, Richard decided upon his plans. To remain in the neighbourhood of the fatal scene, ever again to look upon the Half-moon beach where the dead had lain, he felt would drive him mad. In Australia he might in time find something like rest.

"I shall leave to-night," said he.

"To-night!" echoed Isaac, in great surprise.

Richard nodded. " You will drive me to Jut-point, won't you, Isaac?"

" If you must really go."

" And when shall we see you again?" inquired Mary Anne.

" Never again."

" Never again! never again!" she repeated, with a moan. " Oh Richard, never again!"

It was a shock to Mr. Thornycroft, when he drove home an hour later from Jutpoint, to find his eldest and (as people had looked upon it) his favourite son waiting to bid him farewell for ever. They did not disclose to him the fearful secret—either that it was Cyril who had died, or that it was Richard who had shot him—leaving that to be revealed later. They said Richard had fallen into a serious scrape, which could only be kept quiet by his quitting the place for a few years, and begged him not to inquire particulars; that the less said about it the better. Justice Thornycroft obeyed in his surprise, for the communication had half stunned him.

And so they parted. Once more in the middle of the night—in the little hours interven-ing between dark and dawn—the dogcart was driven out from the Red Court Farm: not bearing this time a quantity of valuable lace or other booty, but simply a portmanteau of Richard's, with a few articles of clothing flung hastily into it.   He sat low down in the seat, his hat over his brows, his arms folded, his silence stern.   And thus Isaac, on the high cushion by his side, drove him to Jutpoint to catch the early morning train.

CHAPTER X.

THE next matter to be disclosed was the marriage of Isaac. It was not done immediately. As the reader may have surmised, the sole cause for his keeping it secret at all had its rise in the smuggling. So long as they ran cargoes into the vaults of the Red Court Farm, so long did Mr. Thornycroft lay an embargo, or wish to lay it, on his sons marrying. The secret might be no longer safe, he said, if one of them took a wife.

With the departure of Richard the smuggling would end. Without him, Mr. Thornycroft would not care to carry it on : and Isaac felt that *he* could never join in it again, after what it had done for Cyril. There was no need : Mr. Thornycroft's wealth was ample. But some weeks went on before Isaac considered himself at liberty to speak.

For the fact was this : Richard Thornycroft

on his departure had extracted a promise from Isaac *not* to disclose particulars until they should hear from him. Isaac gave it readily, supposing he would write before embarking. But the days and the weeks went on, and no letter came: Isaac was at a nonplus, and felt half convinced, in his own mind, that Richard had repented of his determination to absent himself, and would be coming back to Coastdown. With the disclosure of his marriage to the justice, Isaac wished to add another disclosure—that *he* had done with the smuggling for ever; but a fear was upon him that this might lead to a full revelation of the past; and, for Richard's sake, until news should come that he was safe away, Isaac delayed and delayed. His inclination would have been less willing to do this, but for one thing, and that was, that he could not have his wife with him just yet. Mrs. Sam Copp, poor meek Amy, had been seized with a long and dangerous illness. Anna was in close attendance upon her; Mrs. Copp stayed to domineer and superintend; and until she should be better Anna could not leave. Thus the time had gone on, and accident brought about what intention had not.

May was in, and quickly passing. Pretty nearly two months had elapsed since Richard's exit. One bright afternoon when Amy was well enough to sit up at her bed-room window, open to the balmy heath and the sweet breeze from the sparkling sea, Sarah came up and said Mr. Isaac Thornycroft was below. Anna sat with her; the captain and his mother were out.

"May I go down?" asked Anna, with a bright blush.

"I suppose you must, dear," answered Mrs. Sam Copp, with a sigh, given to the long-continued concealment that ever haunted her.

Away went Anna, flying first of all up to her own room to smooth her hair, to see that her pretty muslin dress with its lilac ribbons looked nice. Isaac, under present circumstances, was far more like a lover than a husband : scarcely ever did they see each other alone for an instant. This took her about two minutes, and she went softly downstairs and opened the parlour door.

Isaac was seated with his back to it, on this side the window. Anna, her face in a glow with the freedom of what she was about to do, stepped up, put her hands round his neck from the back, and kissed his hair—kissed it again and again.

" Halloa !" roared out a stern voice.

Away she shrunk, with a startled scream. At the back of the room, having thrown himself on the sofa, tired with his walk, was Captain Copp, his mother beside him. The two minutes had been sufficient time for them to enter. The captain had not felt so confounded since the night of the apparition, and Mrs. Copp's eyes were perfectly round with a broad stare.

" You shameless hussey !" cried the gallant captain, finding his tongue as he advanced. " What on earth——"

But Isaac had risen. Risen, and was taking Anna to his side, holding her up, standing still with calm composure.

" It is all right, Captain Copp. Pardon me. Anna is my wife."

" Your—what ?" roared the captain, really not hearing in his flurry.

" Anna has been my wife since last November. And I hope," Isaac added, with a quiet laugh, partly of vexation, partly of amusement, " that you will give me credit for self-sacrifice and in- finite patience in letting her remain here."

Anna, crying silently in her distress and shame, had turned to him, and was hiding her face on his arm. A minute or two sufficed for the explanation Isaac gave. Its truth could not be doubted, and he finished by calling her a little goose, and bidding her look up. Captain Copp felt uncertain whether to storm or to take it quietly. Meanwhile, he sat down rather humbly, and joined Mrs. Copp in staring.

"A ghost one week; a private marriage the next! I say, mother, I wish I was among the pirates again!"

This discovery decided the question in Isaac's mind, and he went straight to the Red Court to seek a private interview with his father. But he told only of the marriage: leaving other matters to the future. Rather to his surprise, it was well received: Mr. Thornycroft did not say a harsh word.

"Be it so, Isaac. Of business I am thinking we shall do no more. And if I am to be deprived of two of my sons—as appears only too probable—it is well that the third should marry. As to Anna, she is a sweet girl, and I've nothing to say against her, except her want of money. I suppose you considered that you will possess enough for both."

" We shall have enough for comfort, sir."

" And for something else. Go and bring her home here at once, Isaac."

But to this, upon consideration, was raised a decided objection at Captain Copp's. What would the gossips say? Isaac thought of a better plan. He wanted to run up to London for a few days, and would take his wife with him. After their departure, Sarah might be told, who would be safe to go abroad at once and spread the news everywhere: that Miss Chester, under the sanction of her mistress, the captain's wife, had been married in the winter to Isaac Thornycroft.

Mrs. Copp, whose visit had grown to unconscionable length, announced her intention of proceeding with them to London. The captain's wife was quite sufficiently recovered to be left: to use her own glad words, she should " get well all one way," now that the secret was told. So it was arranged, and the captain himself escorted them to Jutpoint.

A gathering at Mrs. Macpherson's. On the day after the arrival in London, that lady had

met the three in the crowd at the Royal
Academy, and invited them at once to her house
in the evening. Isaac, who had seen her once
or twice before, introduced Mrs. Copp, and
whispered the fact that Anna was no longer Miss
Chester, but Mrs. Isaac Thornycroft.

" You'll come early, mind," cried the hospitable wife of the professor. It's just an
ordinary tea-drinking, which is one of the few
good things that if the world means to let die
out, *I* don't; but there'll be some cold meat
with it, if anybody happens to be hungry. The
Miss Jupps are coming, and they dine early.
Tell your wife, Mr. Thornycroft—bless her sweet
face! there's not one to match it in all them
frames—that I'll get in some wedding cake."

Isaac laughed. The jostling masses had left
him behind with Mrs. Macpherson, who was
dressed so intensely high in the fashion, that he
rather winced at the glasses directed to them.
However, they accepted the invitation, and went
to Mrs. Macpherson's in the evening.

Miss Jupp had arrived before them; her
sisters were unable to come. She was looking a
little more worn than usual, until aroused by the
news relating to Anna. Married! and Miss

Jupp had been counting the days, as it were, until she should return to them, for they could not get another teacher like her for patience and work.

Ah, yes: Anna's teaching days were over; her star had brightened. As she sat there in her gleaming silk of pearl-grey, in the golden bracelets, Isaac's gift, with the rose blush on her cheeks, the light of love in her sweet eyes, Mary Jupp saw that she had found her true sphere.

"But, my dear child, why should it have been done in secret?" she whispered.

"There were family reasons," answered Anna, "I cannot tell you now."

"Since last November! Dear me! And was the marriage really not known to any one? was it quite secret?"

"Not quite. One of Isaac's brothers was present in the church to give me away, and Captain Copp's wife knew of it."

"Ah, then you are not to be blamed; I am glad to hear that," sighed Mary Jupp.

"And now tell me, how is my dear Miss Thornycroft?" cried Mrs. Macpherson, as the good professor, in his threadbare coat (rather worse than usual) beguiled Isaac away to his laboratory. " I declare I have not yet asked after her."

Had Mrs. Macpherson been strictly candid, she might have acknowledged to having purposely abstained from asking before Isaac. The fact of the young lady's having got intimate with Robert Hunter at *her* house, and of its being an acquaintance not likely, as she judged, to be acceptable to the Thornycrofts, had rather lain on her mind.

" She looks wretched," answered Mrs. Copp.

" Wretched ?"

" She has fretted all the flesh off her bones. You might draw her through the eye of a needle."

" My patience !" ejaculated Mrs. Macpherson. " The prefessor 'ill be sorry to hear this. What on earth has she fretted over ?"

" That horrible business about Robert Hunter," explained Mrs. Copp. " The justice has not looked like himself since ; and never will again."

" Oh," returned the professor's lady in a subdued tone, feeling suddenly crestfallen. Conscience whispered that this could only apply to the matter she was thinking of, and that the attachment had arisen through her own imprudence in allowing them to meet. She supposed (to use the expressive words passing through her thoughts) that there had been a blow-up.

"It wasn't no fault of mine," she said, after a pause. "Who was to suspect they were going to fall in love with each other in that foolish fashion? She a school-girl, and he an old widower! A couple of spoonies! Other folks as well as me might have been throwed off their guard."

Since Mrs. Macpherson had mixed in refined society she had learnt to speak tolerably well at collected times and seasons. But when flurried her new ideas and associations forsook her, and she was sure to lapse back to the speech of old days.

"Then there *was* an attachment between him and Mary Anne Thornycroft!" exclaimed Mrs. Copp, in a tone of triumph. "Didn't I tell you so, Anna? You need not have been so close about it."

"I do not know that there was," replied Anna. "Mary Anne never spoke of it to me."

"Rubbish to speaking of it," said Mrs. Copp. "You didn't speak about you and Mr. Isaac." Anna bent her head in silence.

" And was there a blow-up with her folks ?"
inquired Mrs. Macpherson, not quite courage-
ously yet. " Miss Jupp! *you* remember—I
come right off to you with my suspicions at the
first moment I had 'em—which was only a day
or so before she went home."

" I don't know about that; there might have
been or there might not," replied Mrs. Copp,
alluding to the question of the " blow-up."
" But I have got my eyes about me, and I can
see how she grieved after him. Why, if there
had been nothing between them, why did she
put on mourning ?" demanded the captain's
mother, looking at the assembled company one
by one.

" She put it on for Lady Ellis," said Anna.

" Oh, did she, though! Sarah told me that
that mourning was on her back before ever Lady
Ellis died. I tell you, I tell you also, ladies,
she put on the black for Robert Hunter."

" Who put on black for him ?" questioned
Mrs. Macpherson, in a puzzle.

" Mary Anne Thornycroft."

" I never heard of such a thing! What did
she do that for ?"

" Why *do* girls do foolish things ?" returned

Mrs. Copp. " To show her respect for him, I suppose."

" A funny way of showing it !" cried Mrs. Macpherson. " Robert Hunter is doing very well where he's gone."

Mrs. Copp turned her eyes on the professor's wife with a prolonged stare.

" It is to be hoped he *is*, ma'am," she retorted, emphatically.

" He is doing so well that his coming back and marrying her wouldn't surprise me in the least. The Thornycrofts won't have no need to set up their backs again him if he can show he is in the way of making his fortune."

" Why, who are you talking of ?" asked Mrs. Copp, after a pause and another gaze.

" Of Robert Hunter. He has gone and left us. Perhaps you did not know it, ma'am ?"

" Yes, I *did*," said Mrs. Copp, with increased emphasis. " Coastdown has too good cause to know it, unfortunately."

This remark caused Mrs. Macpherson to become meek again. " I had a note from him this week," she observed. " It come in a letter to the professor : he sent it me up from his labotory."

The corners of Anna's mouth were gradually lengthening, almost—she could not help the feeling—in a sort of fear. It must be remembered that she knew nothing of the fact that it was not Robert Hunter who had died.

"Perhaps you'll repeat that again, ma'am," said Mrs. Copp, eyeing Mrs. Macpherson in her sternest manner. "You had a note from *him*, Robert Hunter?"

"Yes, I had, ma'am. Writ by himself."

"Where was it written from?"

Mrs. Macpherson hesitated, conscious of her defects in the science of locality. "The professor would know," said she; "I'm not much of a geographer myself. Anyway it come from where he is, somewhere over in t'other hemisphere."

To a lady of Mrs. Copp's extensive travels, round the world a dozen times and back again, the words "over in t'other hemisphere," taken in conjunction with Robert Hunter's known death and burial, conveyed the idea that the celestial hemisphere, and not the terrestrial, was alluded to. She became convinced of one of two things : that the speaker before her was awfully profane, or else mad.

"I know the letters were six weeks reaching us," continued Mrs. Macpherson. "I suppose it would take about that time to get here from the place."

Mrs. Copp pushed her chair back in a heat. "This is the first time I ever came out to drink tea with the insane, and I hope it will be the last," she cried, speaking without reserve, according to her custom. "Ma'am, if you are not a model of profanity, you ought to be in Bedlam."

Mrs. Macpherson wiped her hot face and took out her fan. But she could give as well as take. "It's what I have been thinking of you, ma'am. Do you think *you* are quite right?"

"I right!" screamed Mrs. Copp in a fury. "What do you mean?"

"What do *you* mean?—come!—about me?"

"*That's* plain. I never yet heard of a man, who is dead and gone, writing back letters to his friends. Who brings them? How do they come? Do they drop from the skies or come up through the graves?"

"Lawk a mercy!" cried Mrs. Macpherson, not catching the full import of the puzzling questions. "They come through the post."

Mrs. Copp was momentarily silenced. The

answer was entirely practical: it was not given
in anger; nor, as she confessed to herself, with
any indication of insanity. Light dawned upon
her mind.

"It's the spirits!" she exclaimed, coming to a
sudden conviction. "Well! Before I'd go in
for that fashionable rubbish! A woman of any
pretension to sense believe in *them !*"

"Hang the spirits!" returned Mrs. Macpherson
with offended emphasis. "I'm not quite such a
fool as that. You should hear what the professor says of them. Leastways, not of the
spirits, poor innocent things, which is all delusion,
but of them there rapping mediums that make
believe to call 'em up."

"Then, ma'am, if it's not the spirits you
allude to as bringing the letters, perhaps you'll
explain to me what does bring them."

"What *should* bring them but the post?"

Mrs. Copp was getting angry. "The post
does not bring letters from dead men."

"I never said it did. Robert Hunter's not
dead."

"Robert Hunter *is.*"

"Well, I'm sure!" cried Mrs. Macpherson,
fanning herself.

" Robert Hunter died last January," persisted Mrs. Copp, in excitement. " His unfortunate body lies under the sod in Coastdown church-yard, and his poor restless spirit hovers above it, frightening the people into fits. My son Sam saw it. Isaac Thornycroft saw it."

" Robert Hunter is not dead," fired Mrs. Mac-pherson, who came to the conclusion that she was being purposely deceived; " he is gone to the East to make a railroad. Not that I quite know where the East is," acknowledged she, " or how it stands from this. I tell you all, I got a letter from him, and it was writ about six weeks ago."

" If that lady is not mad, I never was so in-sulted before," cried Mrs. Copp. " I———"

" There must be some mistake," interposed Mary Jupp, who had listened in great surprise. Of herself she could not solve the question, and knew nothing of the movements of Mr. Hunter. But she thought if he were dead that she should have heard of it from his sister Susan. " Perhaps it only requires a word of explanation."

" I don't know what explanation it can require," retorted Mrs. Copp. " The man is dead and buried."

"The man is not," contended Mrs. Macpherson; "he is alive and kicking, and laying down a railroad."

"My son, Captain Copp, was a mourner at his funeral."

" He wrote me a letter six weeks ago, and he wrote one to the professor; and he said he was getting on like a house on fire," doggedly asserted the professor's wife.

"Stay, stay, I pray you," interposed Miss Jupp. "There must be some misunderstanding. You cannot be speaking of the same man."

"We are!" raved both the ladies, losing temper. "It is Robert Hunter, the engineer, who met Mary Anne Thornycroft at my house; and the two—as I suspected—fell in love with each other, which made me very mad."

" And came down to see her at Coastdown, and Susan Hunter was to have come with him, and didn't. Of course we are speaking of the same."

" And I say that he come back from that visit safe and sound, and was in London till April, when he went abroad," screamed Mrs. Macpherson. "He dined here with us the Sunday afore he was off; we had a lovely piece o' the belly o' salmon, and a quarter o' lamb and spring cabbage, and rhubub tart and custards, and a bottle of champagne, that we might drink success to his journey. Very down-hearted he seemed, I suppose at the thoughts of going away; and the next day he started. There! Ask the preffessor, ma'am, and contradict it if you can."

"I won't contradict it," said Mrs. Copp; "I might set on and swear if I did, like my son Sam. You'll persuade me next there's nothing real in the world. Anna Chester—that is, Anna Thornycroft—do you tell what you know. Perhaps they'll hear you."

"Oh, I'll hear the young lady," said Mrs. Macpherson, fanning herself violently; "but nobody can't persuade me that black's white."

Anna quietly related facts, so far as her knowledge extended: Robert Hunter had come to Coastdown, had paid his visit to the Red Court Farm, and on the very night he was to have left for London he was shot as he stood at the edge of the cliffs, fell over, and was not found until the morning—dead!

Her calm manner, impressive in its truth, her minute relation of particulars, her unqualified

assertion that it was Robert Hunter, and could
have been no one else, staggered Mrs. Macpherson.

"And he was shot down dead, you say?"
cried that lady, dropping the fan, and opening
her mouth very wide.

"He must have died at the moment he was
shot. It was not discovered"—here her voice
faltered a little—"who shot him, and the jury
returned a verdict of wilful murder against some
person or persons unknown."

"Was there a inquest?" demanded the
astonished Mrs. Macpherson, "on Robert
Hunter?"

"Certainly there was. He was buried subsequently in Coastdown churchyard. His grave
lies in the east corner of it, near Mrs. Thornycroft's."

"Now you have not told all the truth, Anna,"
burst forth Mrs. Copp, who had been restraining
herself with difficulty. "You are always shuffling
out of that part of the story when you can.
Why don't you say that you and Miss Thornycroft saw him murdered? Tell it as you had to
tell it before the coroner."

"It is true," acknowledged Anna.

"And Miss Thornycroft put on mourning for him, making believe it was for Lady Ellis, who died close upon it," cried Mrs. Copp, too impatient to allow Anna to continue. "And the worst is, that he can't rest in his grave, poor fellow, but hovers atop of it night after night, so that Coastdown dare not go by the churchyard, and the folks have made a way right across the heath to avoid it, breaking through two hedges and a stone fence that belongs to Lord What's-his-name—who's safe, it's said, to indict the parish for trespass. Scores of folks saw the ghost. Anna saw it. My son Sam saw it, and he's not one to be taken in by a ghost; though he did think once he saw a mermaid, and will die, poor fellow, in the belief. Robert Hunter not dead, indeed! He was barbarously murdered, ma'am."

"It is the most astounding tale I ever heard," cried the bewildered Mrs. Macpherson. "What was the ghost like?"

"Like himself, ma'am. Perhaps you knew a coat he had? An ugly white thing garnished with black fur?"

"I had only too good cause to know it!" shrieked out Mrs. Macpherson, aroused at the mention. "That blessed prefessor of mine bought it

and gave it him ; was *took in* to buy it.   He's the
greatest duffer in everyday life that ever stood
upright."

" Then it always appeared in that coat.   For
that was what he had on when he was murdered."

" Well, I never !   I shall think we are in the
world of departed spirits next.   This beats table-
rapping.   Why, he brought that very coat on his
arm when he came on the Sunday to dine with
us !   The nights were cold again."

" And the real veritable coat has been lying
ever since at the public-house where he was
carried to.   It's there now, stiff in its folds,"
eagerly avowed Mrs. Copp.   " Ma'am, what you
saw at your house here must have been a vision—
himself and the coat too."

Mrs. Macpherson began to doubt her own
identity.   The second coat never crossed her
mind.   It happened that she had not looked into
the lumber closet after it, and could have been
upon her oath, if asked, that it was there still.
Her hot face assumed a strange look of dubious
bewilderment.

" It never surely could have been his ghost
that came here and dined with us !" debated she.

"Ghosts don't eat salmon and drink champagne."

" I don't know what they might do if put to it," cried Mrs. Copp, sharply. "One thing you may rely upon, ma'am—that it was not himself."

" The professor doesn't believe in ghosts. He says there is no such things. I'm free to confess that I've never seen any."

" Neither did I believe before this," said Mrs. Copp. "But one has to bend to the evidence of one's senses."

How the argument would have ended, and what they might have brought it to, cannot be divined. Miss Jupp had sat in simple astonishment. That Robert Hunter had died and been buried at Coastdown in January, and that Robert Hunter had dined in that very house in April, appeared absolutely indisputable. It was certainly far more marvellous than any feat yet accomplished by the "spirits." But Isaac Thornycroft solved it.

He came in alone, saying the professor was staying behind to finish some experiment. Upon which the professor's wife went to see, for she did not approve of experiments when there was com-

pany to entertain.   Mrs. Copp immediately began
to recount what had passed, making comments of
her own.

"I have come across many a bum-boat woman
in my day, Mr. Isaac, and I thought they capped
the world for impudent obstinacy, for they'll call
black white to the face of a whole crew.   But
Mrs. Mac beats 'em.   Perhaps you will add your
testimony to mine—that Robert Hunter is dead
and buried.   Miss Jupp here is not knowing
what to think or believe."

Isaac Thornycroft hesitated.   He went and
stood on the hearth-rug in his black clothes.   His
face was grave; his manner betrayed some
agitation.

"Mrs. Copp, will you pardon me if I ask you
generously to dismiss that topic; at least for to-
night?"

"What on earth for?" was the answer of Mrs.
Copp.

"The subject was, and is, and always will be
productive of the utmost pain to my family.
We should be thankful to let all remembrance
of it die out of men's minds."

"Now I tell you what it is, Mr. Isaac; you are
thinking of your brother Cyril.   Of course as

long as he stays away, he'll be suspected of the murder, but I've not said so——"

"Be silent, I pray you," interrupted Isaac, in a tone of sharp pain. "Hear me, while I clear your mind from any suspicion of that kind. By all my hope of heaven—by all *our* hope," he added, lifting solemnly his right hand, "my brother Cyril was innocent."

"Well, we'll let that pass," said Mrs. Copp, with a sniff. "Many a pistol has gone off by accident before now, and small blame to the owners of it. Perhaps you'll be good enough to bear me out to Miss Jupp that Robert Hunter was shot dead."

Isaac paced the room. Mrs. Macpherson had come in and was listening; the professor halted at the door. Better satisfy them once for all, or there would be no end to it.

"It came to our knowledge afterwards—long afterwards—that it was not Robert Hunter," said Isaac, with slow distinctness. "The mistake arose from the face not having been recognisable. Hunter is alive and well."

"The saints preserve us!" cried Mrs. Copp in her discomfiture. "Then why did his ghost appear?"

A momentary smile flitted across the face of Isaac. " I suppose—in point of fact—it was not his ghost, Mrs. Copp."

Mrs. Copp's senses were three-parts lost in wonder at the turn affairs were taking. " Who, then, was shot down ?   A stranger ?"

Isaac raised his handkerchief to his face.   " I daresay it will be known some time. At present it is enough for us that it was not Robert Hunter.'

" I knew a ghost could never eat salmon !" said Mrs. Macpherson, in a glow of triumph.

" But what about the coat ?" burst forth Mrs. Copp, as that portion of the mystery loomed into her recollection.   " If that is lying unusable in the stables at the Mermaid, Robert Hunter could not have brought it with him when he came here to dinner."

Clearly.   And the ladies looked one at another, half inclined to plunge into war again. The meek professor, possibly afraid of it, spoke up in his mild way from behind, where he had stood and listened in silence.

" Mr. Hunter's coat was to have been sent after him from Coastdown ; but it did not come, and I gave him mine. He supposed it must have been lost on the road."

It was the professor's wife's turn now. She could not believe her ears. Give away the other coat—when visions had crossed her mind of having that disreputable fur taken off and decent buttons put on, for his wear the following winter when he went off to the country on his ologies!

" Professor ! do you mean to tell me to my face that that coat is not in the lumber-closet upstairs where I put it?"

" Well, my dear, I fear you'd not find it there."

Away went Mrs. Macpherson to the closet, and away went the rest in her wake, anxious to see the drama played out. Isaac Thornycroft alone did not stir; and his wife came back to him. Her face was white and cold, as though she had received a shock.

" Isaac ! Isaac ! this is frightening me. May I say what I fear ?"

He put his hands upon her shoulders and gazed into her eyes as she stood before him, his own full of kindness but of mourning.

" Say as little as you can, my darling. I can't bear much to-night."

" Cyril ! It—was——"

" Yes."

" Oh, Cyril! Cyril! could he not be saved?"

His faint cry of anguish echoed hers, as he bent his aching brow momentarily upon her shoulder.

" I would have given my own life to save his, Anna. I would give it still to save another the remorse and pain that lie upon him. He put on Hunter's coat that night, the other not wanting it, and was mistaken for him."

" I understand," she murmured. " Oh, what a remorse it must be!"

" Now you know all; but it is for your ear alone," he said, standing before her again and speaking impressively. " From henceforth let it be to us a barred subject, the only one that my dear wife may not mention to me."

She looked an assent from her loving eyes, and sat down again as the company came trooping in, Mrs. Macpherson openly demanding of her husband how long it would be before he learnt common sense, and why he did not cut off his head and give *that* away.

CHAPTER XI.

BACK at Coastdown. Isaac and his wife were staying at the Red Court. Mr. Thornycroft wished them to remain at it altogether; but Isaac doubted. If his sister were to marry, why then he would heartily accede; and Anna could take up her position as its mistress—in anticipation of the period when she would legally be entitled to it. At present he thought it would be better for them to rent a small house near.

Mary Anne had received the news of the marriage with equanimity—not to say apathy. In the dreadful calamities that had overwhelmed her, petty troubles were lost. Cordially indeed did she welcome her brother and his wife home, and hoped they would remain. To be alone there was, as she truly told them, miserable.

A ship letter had been received from Richard,

written when he was nearly half way on his
voyage. It appeared that he had written on embarking, just a word to tell the name of his ship,
and whither it was bound, and had sent it on
shore by the pilot. Isaac could only suppose
that the man had forgotten to post it.

His destination was New Zealand. Some
people whom he knew had settled there, he said,
and he intended to join them. He should pur-
chase some land and farm it; but he would
never again set foot on European soil. He
supposed he should get on ; and he hoped in
time some sort of peace would return to him.

" I would advise your telling my father the
whole, if you have not already done so," the
letter concluded. " It is right that he should
know the truth about Cyril, and that I shall
never come home again. Tell him that the remorse lies very heavily upon me ; that I would
have given my own life ten times over—given it
cheerfully—to save my brother's. Had it been
any one but a brother, I should not feel it so
deeply. I think of myself always as a second
Cain. I will write you again when we arrive.
Meanwhile, address to me at the post-office,
Canterbury. I suppose you will not object to

correspond with me. Perhaps my father will write. Tell him I should like it."

Before the arrival of this letter to Isaac, he had been consulting with his sister about the expediency of enlightening their father. His own opinion entirely coincided with Richard's—that it ought to be done. Mr. Thornycroft was in a state of doubt about Cyril; and also as to the duration of Richard's exile, and restlessly curious always in regard to what had led to it.

One balmy June day, when the crop of hay was being got in, Isaac told his father. They were leaning upon a gate in the four-acre mead, watching the haymakers, who were piling the hay into cocks at the farther end of the field.

Mr. Thornycroft was like a man stunned.

" Hunter not dead ! Cyril lying there, and not Hunter ! It can't *be*, Isaac !"

Isaac repeated the facts again, and then went into details. He concluded by showing Richard's last letter.

" Poor Dicky ! Poor Dicky !" cried the justice, melted to compassion. " Yes, as you say, Isaac, Cyril is in a happier place than this—gone to his rest. And Dick—Dick sent him there in cruelty. I think I'll go in if you'll give me your arm."

Wonderingly Isaac obeyed. Never had the strong, upright Justice Thornycroft sought or needed support from any one. The news must have shaken him terribly. Isaac went with him across the fields, and saw him shut himself in his room.

"Have you been telling him?" whispered Mary Anne.

"Yes."

"And how has he borne it? Why did he lean upon you in coming in?"

"He seemed to bear it exceedingly well. But it must have had a far deeper effect upon him than I thought, or he would not have asked for my arm."

Mary Anne Thornycroft sighed. A little pain, more or less, seemed to her as nothing.

On the following morning Mr. Thornycroft sent for his son. Isaac found him seated before his portable desk; some papers upon it. The crisis of affairs had prompted the justice to disclose certain facts to his children, that otherwise never might have been disclosed. Richard Thornycroft was not his own son, though he had

been treated as such. Isaac listened in utter
amazement. Of all the strange things that had
lately fallen upon them, this appeared to him to
be the strangest.

"I have been writing to Richard," said Mr.
Thornycroft, taking up some closely-written pages.
"You can read it; it will save me going over the
details to you."

Isaac took the letter, and read it through.
But his senses were confused, and it was not very
clear to him.

"It seems that I cannot understand it now,
sir."

"Not understand it?" repeated the justice,
with a touch of his old heat. "It is plain
enough to be understood. When my father died,
he left this place, the Red Court Farm, to my
elder brother, your uncle Richard—whom you
never knew. A short while afterwards, Richard
met with an accident in France, and I went over
with my wife, to whom I was just married. We
found him also with a wife, which surprised me,
for he had never said anything of it; she was a
pretty little Frenchwoman; and their child, a
boy, was a year old. Richard, poor fellow, was
dying, and of course I thought my chance of in-

heriting the Red Court was gone—that he would naturally leave it to his little son. But he took an opportunity of telling me that he had left it to me ; the only proviso attached to it being that I should bring up the boy as my son. He talked with me further : things that I cannot go into now : and I promised. That is how the Red Court came to me."

" But why should he have done this, sir ?" interrupted Isaac, who liked justice better than wrong. " The little boy had a right to it."

" No," said Mr. Thornycroft, quietly. " Richard had not married his mother."

Isaac saw now. There was a pause.

" He said if time could come over again he would have married her, or else not have taken her. He was dying, you see, Isaac, and right and wrong array themselves in very distinct colours then. Anyway, it was too late now, whatever his repentance ; and he prayed me and my wife to take the boy and not let it be known for the child's own sake that he was not ours. We both promised ; at a moment like that one could not foresee inconveniences that might arise later, and it almost seemed as if we owed the compliance, in gratitude for the bequeathal of the

Red Court Farm. He died, and we brought the boy with us to London—he who has been looked upon as your brother Richard. When people here used to say that he was more like his uncle Richard than his father Harry, my wife would glance at me with a smile."

"And his mother?"

"She died in France shortly afterwards. She had parted with the boy readily, glad to find he would have so good a home. Had she lived, the probabilities are that the secret could not have been kept."

"Did you intend to keep it always, father?"

"Until my death. Every year as they went on, gave less chance of our disclosing it. When you were all little, my wife and I had many a serious consultation; for the future seemed to be open to some difficulty; but we loved the boy, and neither of us had courage to say, He is not ours; he has no legitimate inheritance. Besides, as your mother would say to me, there was always our promise. It must have been disclosed at my death, at least to Richard, to explain why you, and not he, came into the Red Court."

"Perhaps his father, my uncle Richard, expected it would be left to him?"

"No, Isaac. We talked of that. Only in the event of my having no children of my own would the property have become his. Richard will take his share as one of my younger children. *You* are the eldest. I shall at once settle this money upon him ; you have read to that effect in the letter ; so that he will have enough for comfort whatever part of the world he may choose to remain in."

Isaac mechanically cast his eyes on the letter, still in his hand.

" I have disclosed these facts to him now for his own comfort," resumed Mr. Thornycroft. " It may bring him a ray of it to find Cyril was not his brother."

Isaac thought it would. He folded the letter and returned it to his father.

"There is one thing I wished to ask you, sir, and I may as well ask it now. You do not, I presume, think of running more cargoes."

" Never again," said Mr. Thornycroft. " Richard was the right hand of it, and he is gone. That's over for ever. But for him it would have been given up before. And there's Kyne besides."

Isaac nodded, glad to have the matter set at rest.

"May I tell Mary Anne what you have disclosed to me?"

"Yes, but no one else. She may be glad to hear Richard is not her brother."

How glad, the justice little thought. It seemed to Mary Anne as if this news removed the embargo she had self-imposed upon her marriage with Robert Hunter. Perhaps she had already begun to question the necessity of it—to think it a very utopian, severe decision. In the revulsion of feeling that came over her, she laid her head down on Isaac's shoulder with a burst of tears, and told him all. Isaac smiled.

"You must tell him that you have relented, Mary Anne."

"He will not be back for five years."

"He will be back in less than five months; perhaps in five weeks."

She sat upright, staring at him.

"Isaac!"

"He will, indeed. Anna had a letter from him yesterday. It came to Miss Jupp's, addressed to 'Miss Chester.' Business matters are bringing him home for a short while; personal things, he says, that only himself can do. I wonder if he wrote to her in the hope that the information would penetrate to Coastdown?"

She sat in silence, her colour going and coming, rather shrinking from the merriment in Isaac's eye. Oh, would it be so?—would it be so?

" In that case—I mean, should circumstances bring him again to the Red Court Farm—we shall have to disclose publicly the truth about Cyril, Mary Anne. As well that it should be so, and then a tombstone can be put. But it can wait yet."

As she sat there, looking out on the sparkling sea, a prevision came over her that this happiness might really come to her at last, and a sobbing sigh of thankfulness went up to heaven.

Coastdown went on in its ordinary quiet routine. The mysteries of the Red Court Farm were at an end, never again to be enacted. Long and perseveringly did Mr. Superintendent Kyne look out for the smugglers; many and many a night did he exercise his eyes and his patience on the edge of that bleak plateau; but they came no more. Old Mr. Thornycroft, deprived, he hardly knew how, of his sons, lived on at the

Red Court, feeling at times a vacancy of pursuit:
he had loved adventure, and his occupation was
gone. But the land got a better chance of being
tilled to perfection now than it ever had been.

Meanwhile the whole neighbourhood remained
under a clear and immutable persuasion that
the ghost still "walked" in the churchyard.
The new right of road had come to a hot dis-
pute; but Coastdown persisted in using it after
nightfall, to avoid the graves and their ominous
visitor. While Captain Copp, taking his glass in
the parlour at the Mermaid, did not fail to
descant upon the marvels of that night, when
he and that woman-servant of his, who (he
would add in a parenthesis) was undaunted
enough for a she-pirate, saw with their own eyes
the spirit of Robert Hunter. And then the parlour would fall into a discussion of the love of
roving inherent in the young Thornycrofts—
Cyril lingering away still; Richard also—perhaps gone to look after him; and speculate
upon how long it would be before they returned,
and the glorious dinners were resumed at the
Red Court Farm.

THE END.

TINSLEY BROTHERS' NEW WORKS.

NOTICE.

The Life of David Garrick. From Original
Family Papers. and numerous Published and Unpublished Sources.
By PERCY FITZGERALD, M.A. 2 vols. 8vo, with Portraits.

"Once taken up, it will not be easily laid down. Unquestionably, it is the most
satisfactory biography that has yet appeared of our English Roscius."—*Examiner.*

"It is very interesting; its annals and anecdotes will be pleasant to many who rise
unrefreshed from the reading of a portentous novel."—*Standard.*

"Everyone, either professiona'ly or generally interested in the stage, should read
the 'Life of David Garrick.' It will be found full of information, well stocked with
valuable suggestions, and wonderfully interesting."—*Globe.*

"Mr Fitzgerald is fairly entitled to be considered the only writer who has yet given
us a 'Life of Garrick' worthy to be so called."—*Leader.*

"Mr. Fitzgerald has evidently been thoroughly painstaking in the collection and
collation of his facts; and the result is that we have for the first time a really valuable
history of David Garrick."—*Star.*

"Pleasant reading in itself, and does credit to Mr. Fitzgerald's industry. We may
recommend these volumes to the lovers of Biography, and especially to lovers of the
lives of actors."—*Athenæum.*

"We have, at last, a biography of the reformer of the British stage in the 18th century, filled with amusing anecdote, and pleasant reminiscences."—*Bell's Weekly
Messenger.*

Con Amore; or Chapters on Criticism. By the
Author of "The Waterdale Neighbours." In 1 vol.

THE STATE OF IRELAND.

A Saxon's Remedy for Irish Discontent. In
1 vol. 9s.

The Law: What I have Seen, What I have
Heard, and What I have Known. By CYRUS JAY. In 1 vol.
7s. 6d.

Notes and Sketches of the Paris Exhibition.
By G. A. SALA, Author of "My Diary in America," &c. In 1 vol.
15s.

TINSLEY BROTHERS, 18, CATHERINE STREET, STRAND.

TINSLEYS' MAGAZINE,

An Illustrated Monthly,

Price One Shilling.

CONDUCTED BY EDMUND YATES,

CONTAINS :

BREAKING A BUTTERFLY ; OR, BLANCHE ELLERSLIE'S ENDING. By the Author of "GUY LIVINGSTONE," &c.

A HOUSE OF CARDS. A NOVEL. By a New Writer.

NOVELS : By EDMUND YATES, Author of "BLACK SHEEP," &c., WILLIAM HOWARD RUSSELL, LL.D., of the *Times.*

&c. &c. &c.

. *Published in the middle of every month.*

NOTICE.

A New Novel by the Author of "East Lynne," "Mrs. Haliburton's Troubles," "Lord Oakburn's Daughters," "St. Martin's Eve," &c.

The Red Court Farm. By Mrs. HENRY WOOD,
Author of "East Lynne," "Trevlyn Hold," "Mildred Arkell," &c. 3 vols.

The Rock Ahead : A New Novel. By EDMUND
YATES, Author of "Black Sheep," "Kissing the Rod," &c. 3 vols.

John Haller's Niece : a Novel. By RUSSELL
GRAY, Author of "Never—for Ever." 3 vols.

Brakespeare ; or, The Fortunes of a Free Lance.
By the Author of "Guy Livingstone," "Sword and Gown," &c. 3 vols.

The Adventures of Dr. Brady. By W. H.
RUSSELL, LL.D. 3 vols. Second Edition.

The Dower House. The New Novel. By ANNIE
THOMAS (Mrs. PENDER CUDLIP), Author of "Called to Account," &c. 3 vols.

Sorrow on the Sea. A New Novel. By Lady
WOOD, Author of "Sabina," &c. 3 vols.

Martyrs to Fashion. A Novel. By JOSEPH
VEREY. 3 vols.

TINSLEY BROTHERS, 18, CATHERINE STREET, STRAND.

TINSLEY BROTHERS'
CHEAP EDITIONS OF POPULAR NOVELS.

BY MRS. J. H. RIDDELL, Author of "George Geith," &c.

Far Above Rubies. 6s.   Phemie Keller. 6s.
The Race for Wealth. 6s.   Maxwell Drewitt. 6s.
George Geith. 6s.   Too Much Alone. 6s.
The Rich Husband. 6s.   City and Suburb. 6s.

BY MRS. HENRY WOOD, Author of "East Lynne," &c.

Elster's Folly. 6s.   Mildred Arkell. 6s.
St. Martin's Eve. 6s.   Trevlyn Hold. 6s.

BY THE AUTHOR OF "GUY LIVINGSTONE."

Sword and Gown. 2s.   Maurice Dering. 6s.
Barren Honour. 2s.   Guy Livingstone. 5s.

Also, now ready, Uniform with the above.

Black Sheep. By EDMUND YATES, Author of "The Rock Ahead," &c. 6s.

Not Wisely, but Too Well. A Novel. By the Author of "Cometh up as a Flower." 6s.

Lizzy Lorton of Greyrigg. By Mrs. LYNN LINTON, Author of "Sowing the Wind," &c. 6s.

Archie Lovell. By the Author of "The Morals of Mayfair," &c. 6s.

Miss Forrester. By the Author of "Archie Lovell," &c. 6s.

Recommended to Mercy. By the Author of "Sink or Swim?" 6s.

The Savage Club Papers (1867). With all the original Illustrations. 2s.

TINSLEY BROTHERS, 18, CATHERINE STREET, STRAND.

PRICE SIXPENCE, MONTHLY.

MRS. HENRY WOOD'S MAGAZINE,

THE ARGOSY.

EDITED BY MRS. HENRY WOOD.

Contents of the First Number, New Series.

Contents of the January Number.

Contents of the February Number.

Contents of the March Number.

Contents of the April Number.

Price SIXPENCE, MONTHLY,

OF ALL BOOKSELLERS IN THE KINGDOM.